THE HIGH HOUSE

THE HIGH HOUSE

Honor Arundel

Illustrated by
Eileen Armitage

CANONGATE KELPIES

First published 1967 by Hamish Hamilton
First published in Kelpies 1993

Copyright © Honor Arundel
Illustrations © Eileen Armitage
Cover illustration by Alexa Rutherford

British Library Cataloguing-in-Publication Data
A catalogue record for this book is available
on request from the British Library.

ISBN 0 86241 420 2

Printed and bound in Denmark by Norhaven A/S

CANONGATE PRESS, 14 FREDERICK STREET,
EDINBURGH EH2 2HB

Chapter One

AUNT PATSY arrived the morning after the accident and as she had always lived in Edinburgh and we had always lived in London and neither of us had had enough money for the fares, we had never met her before.

She was Mother's sister, tall and thin, with dark straight hair so smooth it looked polished, grey eyes, a pointed nose and long nervous hands. She came on the overnight train and arrived just as Richard and I were thinking about breakfast. I say thinking because we both knew we couldn't eat. But I boiled an egg for Aunt Patsy and made some tea and she ate and drank in an absent-minded way. She hadn't said much. She hugged us when she arrived but without kissing – I hate the way most relations think they have the right to kiss you whether you know and like them or not.

She was quite different from Aunt Laura, Father's sister, who arrived with Uncle Edward from their home in Exeter later in the morning and immediately took charge.

Aunt Laura was square and brisk and she wore

a black suit and a black hat (Aunt Patsy was wearing green corduroy and no hat) but she looked as if she would be more at home in baggy country tweeds.

Uncle Edward, who was a lawyer, was also square and brisk, with rimless glasses and thin grey hair. They both kissed us and Aunt Laura cried and called us 'poor little orphans' and kept repeating, 'It's so terrible. I can't believe it. I just can't believe it.'

Mother and Father had been killed in a car smash on their way home from visiting friends. I can't write about it.

As I said, Aunt Laura took charge; she sent Richard and me upstairs to rest and bustled into the kitchen, clattering things. Uncle Edward settled beside the telephone and Aunt Patsy was left in the living-room, smoking, and staring out of the window.

Richard and I crept upstairs but we didn't seem able to rest. Instead, we went into Richard's room and Richard stood by the window kicking the carpet and I sat on the divan. Sometimes, when something terrible has happened you can't feel it. It's like cutting yourself really badly. At first it doesn't feel at all and then very gradually it begins to ache. We were still at the numb stage.

Richard is fifteen, two years older than me. He is tall for his age and he has dark copper-coloured hair and lots of freckles. My hair's the same colour

but somehow I have escaped the freckles. He is a terribly nice brother and quite unlike most boys you meet because he doesn't show off or think he's a superior person just because he's a boy. He is going to be a musician. But the best thing about him is that he always knows how I feel and never laughs when I say stupid things accidentally.

I remember that bit of the morning very clearly, the sound of Aunt Laura in the kitchen, the bumble of Uncle Edward on the telephone and the sound of bird-song coming through the open window.

We live in a fairly new suburb and there aren't many trees big enough to be called proper trees, but there is one which must have been there already, a sycamore, a lovely round symmetrical tree and it's at the bottom of our garden. Every now and again some stupid neighbour wants to cut it down but we won't let him. That morning, it was early September, the tree was just beginning to turn yellow and every now and again a leaf would be blown off and fall very gently on to the grass. And this seemed very sad although the sun was shining. On any other day it wouldn't have seemed sad at all because I love autumn.

At last I said: 'If we're orphans will we have to go into a Home?'

'I don't know,' Richard said.

Somehow saying the word 'orphans' made me want to cry for the first time.

'Perhaps one of the aunts will take us,' Richard went on.

I simply couldn't think clearly what that would be like. My head ached and my eyes ached – we'd been up most of the night – and I felt tired with that dreadful dragging sort of tiredness which stops you going to sleep. But I longed to sleep and

sleep and then wake up to find it had all been a terrible dream.

Then Aunt Patsy knocked at the door and came in. We didn't want to talk to her at all but she said we must: it was only fair that we should know what was happening.

9

'Have we got to go into a Home?' I asked.

'Homes aren't so horrible nowadays, more like boarding schools,' Aunt Patsy said with the ghost of a smile. 'Not like Oliver Twist at all. But there is an alternative.'

'You mean we could live with you or Aunt Laura?' Richard said.

'I wish you both could but I simply haven't room. And Aunt Laura can't afford it. But she says she'll take Richard if I take you, Emma.'

'You mean we couldn't be together?' I asked horrified.

'That's what I want to talk about. If you went to some sort of a Home you could be together.'

'What about a boarding school?' said Richard.

'Too expensive, at the moment anyhow. But it might be managed later.'

'So it's a choice,' said Richard gloomily, looking down at his feet. 'Together in some ghastly Home or separately with the aunts.'

'Yes. I thought you ought to choose. Aunt Laura's boy, Colin, is just about your age, Richard, so you would have someone to do things with.'

'He was a horrible boy last time I saw him.'

'Most boys grow out of being horrible,' said Aunt Patsy. 'I know it's difficult to choose, especially at a time like this. And especially for Emma because she's never met me before. But there's a spare room in my flat and there are lots of nice things to do in Edinburgh. I'm untidy and bad-tempered and I'm used to living on my own, but we could try it as a temporary arrangement. If you hate it too much or I hate it too much we'll have to think of something else.'

I liked her saying that, I mean not pretending that she loved me or promising to make me happy or saying she would be a second mother. I didn't want another mother. I felt I ought to thank her or something but I just couldn't.

'Well, what do you think?' Aunt Patsy asked. 'Or do you want to talk it over?'

I looked at Richard and Richard looked at me. My look said, 'Please not a Home, I couldn't bear it,' and Richard's look said, 'I'll put up with Aunt Laura if you put up with Aunt Patsy.'

'OK,' said Richard slowly, 'I'll give Aunt Laura a try.'

Aunt Patsy smiled again, this time a proper smile. She wanted to say something cheering or comforting, I knew, but what was there to say? She went towards the door and then turned and said :

'You know, nothing stays the same. We won't always feel like this.'

At this I started to cry and lay on Richard's bed and stuck my head in the pillow. The numbness had gone and the ache I had been expecting was so sudden and so dreadful that I felt there weren't enough tears in the world to drown it.

I don't remember anything about the rest of the day, or rather I don't want to remember. I just remember the sycamore tree and the leaves falling off, sadly, one by one.

Chapter Two

AUNT PATSY and I arrived at Waverley Station, Edinburgh, about seven o'clock in the morning. I realized that she was the sort of person who feels cross and prickly in the early morning so I didn't say much and neither did she except 'I hope you managed to sleep' and 'We'd better get a taxi.'

A strange town looks twice as strange first thing in the morning with no one about and I felt too blurred and excited and confused to notice anything except the coldness and freshness of the air and the cold grey tall buildings. The taxi drove up a steep hill and then turned right and went on climbing.

'I live near the Castle,' said Aunt Patsy. 'It's the oldest part of Edinburgh.'

When we got out I realized what she meant. The buildings were all tall and twisty and some of them looked as though they would fall down at any moment. I couldn't imagine how anyone could live in them and said so.

'Well, I do,' said Aunt Patsy, a little sharply, as she paid the cab driver.

'How are you going to manage with the trunk,

lady?' he asked, slamming the door behind us.

'I'll take one end,' said Aunt Patsy, and to my horror she and the cab driver began walking down a flight of stone steps beside one of these huge crumbling buildings, carrying my trunk between them, leaving me to follow with the suitcases. I couldn't think where they were going. Surely Aunt Patsy couldn't live here?

I paused for a moment at the top of the steps and looked blearily down. At the bottom a wide road curled round like a snake and then more steps went down another hill until they disappeared among hundreds of tall dark buildings, all with puffing chimneys.

I walked slowly down the steps and joined Aunt Patsy and the cab driver who had put the trunk down outside a shabby-looking red door.

'We'll leave it at the foot of the stairs and I'll get it carried up later,' said Aunt Patsy, who didn't even seem to be panting.

'How far up are you?' asked the cab driver.

'Fourth floor,' said Aunt Patsy.

He eyed the trunk doubtfully and then shrugged his shoulders.

'I'll do it,' he said, 'though it'll probably be the death of me.'

It'll probably be the death of me too, I thought, as Aunt Patsy opened the door and led the way into what looked and smelt like a cellar.

The cab driver managed to hoist the trunk on to

his shoulder (of course, it wasn't a very big trunk but still!) and set off after Aunt Patsy up the winding stone stairs, and I brought up the rear. The paint was peeling off the walls, one of the stair windows was broken and the steps had great sags worn in the middle of them. I felt gloomier and gloomier – I mean, this was practically a slum.

I was panting a bit myself because the suitcases were jolly heavy and the stairs seemed to go on for ever but we finally stopped at a blue door with P. Grieve written on a brass plate.

The driver up-ended the trunk and mopped his brow.

'They stairs'll keep you fit,' he grunted.

'They do,' said Aunt Patsy smiling.

Aunt Patsy opened the door, gave the cab driver some more money, told him he was an angel, told me to dump the cases anywhere and began pottering round the flat the way people do when they have been away, picking up letters and newspapers and putting them down again and wandering about in a clueless way.

Inside, the flat wasn't too bad, at least nothing like as bad as I had thought it would be judging from the stairs, but it was still pretty weird. And I realized that she'd not been joking when she said she was untidy because the whole flat was in a frightful mess.

Off the hall was the kitchen and the sink was full of washing-up that hadn't been done and generally littered with odds and ends; then came the bathroom which was tiny, and then Aunt Patsy's bedroom with the bed unmade and lots of clothes and stockings lying about.

'This will be your room,' said Aunt Patsy opening another door.

I nearly died. It had obviously been used as a junk room and though there was a divan bed and a chest of drawers there were no curtains or carpet. And everywhere was junk, piles of books, an umbrella, a broken table lamp, a deck chair and a sewing machine.

'It's in a bit of a mess,' said Aunt Patsy offhandedly, 'but we'll soon have it shipshape.'

'How? When?' I wanted to ask but I felt too miserable to speak. I thought of our lovely house in London, all clean and new and tidy, and my lovely room with the curtains I had chosen myself and my desk and my bookcase. It was terribly difficult not to sit down and howl.

Aunt Patsy must have realized a little of what I was feeling because she said:

'We'll make it nice, I promise. And we'll get the things you specially like sent up from London. Now come and see my studio.'

She led the way up a little flight of stairs into a huge room, a sort of attic with slopey ceilings and two skylights as well as dormer windows. It was all painted white and had a wooden polished floor with shabby rugs on it. There were dozens of pictures, mostly unframed and pinned with drawing pins, and curious lumps of stone that could have been anything and a stone jar full of dead brown hemlock.

And untidy – I couldn't imagine how anyone could live in such a room. There was a piano with stacks of music just about to fall off the top. There was a long thin table covered with papers and books and coffee cups and ashtrays. There was a sofa and a couple of ancient armchairs that looked as though they would collapse if you sat on them. And one half of the room was full of painting things, an easel, stacks of paper and canvases, a drawing board, bottles of this and that and jugs full of paintbrushes and pencils. (Aunt Patsy is the sort of artist who does illustrations for books and magazines and designs for dress materials and things like that.) I remembered that Mother had said she was 'artistic', and now I knew what she meant.

'Come and look at the view, Emma,' said Aunt Patsy. 'Isn't it marvellous?'

You must have been able to see the whole of Edinburgh from those windows, miles and miles of buildings and trees, low hills (which Aunt Patsy said were called 'the Pentlands') and even what looked like the sea in the distance.

'That's the Forth,' said Aunt Patsy.

And bang in front was a wide square, at the far end of which was a gaunt rocky lump with houses and towers on it.

'That's the Castle and the Esplanade. Well, what do you think of my house?'

I decided not to say what I really thought, that

it was weird and horrible and badly needed tidying up and that I couldn't imagine how I would ever settle down there.

'I never imagined it would be like this,' I said lamely. 'Are all Edinburgh houses like this? I mean, aren't there any new houses?'

'Of course. As I told you, this is the oldest part of the city. But I love it. I hate little modern match-boxes.'

I had thought that perhaps a modern house would be too expensive, because I knew she hadn't much money, but to think of anyone choosing to live in a place like this!

I turned away from the window. The view was really too much of a good thing: it made me feel dizzy and overwhelmed and lonely. I'd rather have had a sycamore tree than a castle any day.

'What we need is some breakfast,' said Aunt

Patsy suddenly. 'Oh dear, there isn't a thing in the house.'

We went down to the kitchen again and she poked about in a cupboard and looked in the fridge. 'Not a thing!' she said, but not as if she were surprised or sorry. 'I'll tell you what, Emma, I'll put the kettle on and you run down to the dairy for milk and eggs and some morning rolls.'

She gave me a latch key and a ten-shilling note and I climbed down the four flights of stairs and then up the steps into the main street. I was certainly going to get plenty of exercise in Edinburgh, I thought bitterly. I'd probably wear my legs to stumps.

I found the dairy quite easily and bought the things Aunt Patsy had asked for. I wondered if she had Nescafé, which I always like for breakfast, and decided she might easily not, so I bought a small tin.

The street was beginning to wake up and look more cheerful, but I couldn't get used to those tall black buildings, and when I thought of our nice tree-lined streets and little houses with gardens it was even worse.

When I got back (down the steps and up the stairs) Aunt Patsy had cleared the table and put out mugs and plates and butter and marmalade.

'I didn't know if you had Nescafé so I got some,' I said. 'I hope that's all right.'

'You're a very intelligent girl, Emma,' said Aunt Patsy and she smiled, a really warm smile as if, for the first time, she thought she might like me. I smiled back.

'Here's your change,' I said. 'I wrote down what everything cost and it came to—'

Aunt Patsy interrupted. 'For goodness sake,' she said impatiently. 'I can't add up, and life's too short to count change.'

'But—' I was really shocked. I had been keeping accounts for years whenever I did shopping for Mother; she was most strict about every penny and said it was good training.

'Let's eat a huge breakfast and then we'll make plans. There's a terrible lot to do. You'll have to tell me all sorts of things—' Her voice trailed away. 'I mean I haven't the faintest idea what girls of your age should do or wear or eat or what they like or anything.'

'First I shall clear out my room,' I said firmly.

'Yes, of course. Put all the junk outside the front door and I'll arrange for the dustmen to collect it. There are clean sheets in the airing cupboard. Then we'd better paint the walls – is there any special colour you'd like? Tell me and I'll go out and buy some emulsion paint. Then we'll measure the windows and you can choose curtain material. I wish I could afford a carpet but I won't be able to until I get a pretty fat cheque. But we might manage a rug. Can you use a sewing machine?'

'Yes,' I said. Mother believed in girls being able to sew and cook and things like that.

'Oh good, because I never can remember how to thread up the wretched thing.'

Just then the phone rang and I heard Aunt Patsy say: 'Of course. Do come to lunch and meet my nice niece.'

Honestly! Think of asking someone to lunch on a day like this.

While Aunt Patsy talked to the voice at the other end of the telephone, I stacked the dishes in the sink. At least I could get the washing-up out of the way.

Chapter Three

WHEN I had finished washing up and put everything away – probably in the wrong places – and mopped the floor, I surveyed the wreckage of the room that was going to be mine. Aunt Patsy had disappeared. I hoped she was tidying the studio.

First I cleared out all the junk and stacked it neatly outside the front door. This left the divan, a chest of drawers, a rather saggy basket chair, a sort of ottoman thing and a table. Then I swept the floor, dusted and washed down the paintwork. It certainly made a faint improvement.

Aunt Patsy wandered in at this point.

'I'm going out to do the shopping,' she said. 'My, what a transformation! You're a genius, Emma.'

I looked at her sourly.

'Where shall I put the things from the chest of drawers? And is there any clean shelf paper?'

'Use newspaper,' said Aunt Patsy. 'And put the things – oh anywhere. In the ottoman for the moment.'

'That's full too.'

'Oh dear. Well, put them on my bed and I'll go through them and chuck out what I can. How does one accumulate so much stuff? You know, Emma, you're exactly like Christine.'

I couldn't help flinching to hear my mother's name but Aunt Patsy went on:

'We used to share a room when we were little and I used to drive her mad with my untidiness. We used to draw a chalk line down the middle of the floor and if she found any of my things on her side she used to kick them over the line, but she wouldn't pick them up. I can see I'm going to drive you mad too.'

'I like things to be tidy,' I mumbled.

'You're absolutely right. But don't try to reform me, I'm past redemption. What is in the chest of drawers, by the way?' She flung open a drawer. 'Oh, photographs. You must look.'

She took out the drawer and sat on the divan.

'Look, here we are in our ghastly school uniforms. And this was on a picnic in the Pentlands. And this is Granny, doesn't she look a scream?'

She handed me photo after photo, exclaiming and laughing. I daresay she didn't mean to be cruel but every time she said 'Christine' or 'your mother' it was like walking on knives. Suddenly she noticed I was crying.

'Emma, I didn't mean to upset you. But you see, we had such jolly times when we were children and I like to remember them.

'We'll look at them some other time. Now I must fly and don't bother with the rest of the room if you're tired. What colour paint shall I get? White?'

I nodded. What did it matter what colour my room was? Aunt Patsy disappeared and I heard the front door click.

I lay back on the divan and remembered too. I remembered Mother reading to me when I was ill in bed in her special reading-aloud voice; and Father coming home from work saying 'Surprise' because he'd brought us sweets or flowers; and how we'd all sit and plan summer holidays, whether we'd go to a farm in Devon or a seaside cottage in Cornwall or climb mountains in North Wales; and the time Richard fell off his bicycle and broke his arm – and then the door bell rang.

Honestly! Aunt Patsy! Here was a strange person coming to lunch and she was out and I was in a ghastly mess and feeling like death.

I ran a comb through my hair, and rubbed a dust mark off my face with a handkerchief before I opened the door. There was a strange man outside and for a moment I stared at him blankly. Then I remembered my manners. (Mother had always been particularly keen about good manners.)

'Won't you come in?' I said as graciously as I could. 'Aunt Patsy's gone to do the shopping. I'm Emma Langham, her niece.'

'Hullo, niece Emma. My name's Stephen McTaggart and I've been invited to lunch.'

He was rather crummily dressed in a navy donkey jacket and scuffed suede shoes, and he wore a dark-green jersey instead of a shirt and tie. He had light-blue eyes, a crooked sort of nose and his smile showed rather bad teeth.

'I'll hang up your jacket,' I said and then he followed me upstairs to the studio. He used a lot of swear words when he talked but I won't put them in.

'Typical of Patsy to be out. She has no more sense of time than a seagull. I hope she hasn't forgotten she invited me to lunch,' he went on as he sank heavily into an armchair. 'And what about offering me a drink? I'm as thirsty as a camel. What do you think of Edinburgh? Have you come to stay for long?'

So Aunt Patsy hadn't even told him about me and of course she hadn't tidied the studio.

'I don't know where she keeps the drinks,' I said disapprovingly. Mother and Father never had a drink before lunch except a glass of sherry on Sundays.

'Well I do, if you'll get the glasses from the kitchen.'

I fled downstairs carrying two empty coffee cups and an ashtray, and looked for glasses. I wasn't sure what he was going to drink so I brought two tumblers, in case it was beer, and two small glasses, in case it was sherry.

Actually he wanted gin and vermouth.

'How about you?' he asked.

'I don't drink.'

'Try a little vermouth.'

'No, thank you.'

'Mum disapprove?'

To my horror I burst into tears. 'My mother's dead – that's why I'm here,' I managed to blurt out.

He was as nice as possible or tried to be. He gave me his handkerchief and insisted upon my trying some vermouth which didn't taste too horrible after all.

'I'm terribly sorry, Emma, behaving like a clown, when you must be feeling wretched. Now drink up like a good girl and forgive me.

'So you're coming to live here? I think that'll be an excellent thing for Patsy, she's getting eccentric from living alone and I can see you're going to be a thoroughly good influence on her. You'll settle down in no time. Edinburgh's a great place to live. Are you interested in history? If you are I'll show you one or two places.'

Actually, history is one of the things I am interested in so I said Yes, that would be very kind of him.

Then he started telling me about the Old Town and all the famous people who had lived there, poets and philosophers and artists and scientists, so that by the time Aunt Patsy arrived I had more or less recovered.

She burst into the room carrying two string bags bursting with shopping, a bottle of wine, a bunch of flowers and a long loaf of French bread.

Mr McTaggart got up and kissed her.

'My poor Patsy,' he said. 'You should have told me.'

For a minute Aunt Patsy's face looked as though she might cry too, but then she smiled.

'This is going to be a special lunch to welcome Emma. We're not going to be sad.' Then she turned to me. 'Would you like to get some knives and forks and plates and things and bring them up and we'll eat in here.'

While I was downstairs I washed my face and brushed my hair and put on a clean jersey and then rummaged in the kitchen. I was glad I had done the washing-up.

Aunt Patsy had brought a cold chicken and tomatoes and little cartons of salady things and a chocolate cake. Mr McTaggart was opening a bottle of pink wine, and he poured some into three glasses.

'We're going to drink to you, Emma,' he said. 'Welcome to Edinburgh!'

It seemed a funny sort of lunch to invite someone to, it was more like a picnic really. At home when we had visitors we always had everything very nice, flowers and the best table mats and butter knives and matching plates and coffee afterwards in tiny cups.

I didn't talk much but Aunt Patsy and Mr McTaggart chattered away about all sorts of people and things and about their work – it turned out he was the Art Editor of a magazine she sometimes worked for – and they used a lot of words and technical terms I didn't understand. Every now and again they tried to bring me into the conversation but it was difficult because they didn't know what to say to me and I couldn't think of anything to say to them. Although the chicken was very nice I wasn't hungry. Suddenly I felt dreadfully tired. Too much had been happening too quickly and it was as if my brain had stopped and refused to think a single other thought. I sat curled up in one of the shabby armchairs and my eyes just wouldn't keep open although I knew it was terribly rude to fall asleep in company.

Then Mr McTaggart noticed me.

'Patsy, that poor child is dropping with fatigue. Do something about it.'

I blinked.

'Come on, Emma,' said Aunt Patsy. 'Trot off and have a sleep.'

'But I haven't made my bed,' I mumbled.

'You can use mine.'

I meant to explain and apologize but it was too difficult. I let Aunt Patsy take me into her room and turn down the bed and draw the curtains.

'I'll wake you up at tea-time,' she said as I took off my skirt so that it wouldn't get crushed.

'But I never sleep in the daytime.'

'It's different when you've been travelling all night.'

My eyes were shut almost before she was out of the door.

Chapter Four

I WOKE up very slowly as if I had been wrapped in swathes of cotton wool and it had to be moved away bit by bit. I kept my eyes shut for a long time after I was actually awake and tried to sort out where I was and what I was going to do. I always like to do this when I wake up so that I can remind myself to take gym shoes or a tennis racket to school or take a last look at my French verbs or check a history date. Now I was remembering slowly and painfully that I was in Edinburgh, that my room was still in a mess, and that Aunt Patsy would probably still be sitting upstairs talking to Mr McTaggart. I wondered what time it was.

But she wasn't. She and Mr McTaggart were in my room; he was standing on a chair rollering the ceiling and she was sloshing emulsion paint on to the walls with a big brush. She was wearing an old green shirt instead of an overall and her head was tied up in a duster.

'Ever done any painting, Emma?' she asked. 'If so you'll find an old shirt in my room and you can do the window and the door. I've got the non-drip sort of paint but if you should spill any mop it up quickly before it dries.'

She showed me how to do the windows, starting with the insides in the top left-hand corner and leaving the outsides till the end, and how to take a little piece of rag to wipe off any paint on the glass. It was pretty tricky and I got a crick in my neck twisting myself into knots to see into the corners but, in a way, I was enjoying myself. We didn't talk much but Mr McTaggart kept swearing when he put too much paint on the roller and it sprayed into his eyes, and in between he sang songs which I liked although they were Scotch and difficult to understand.

At last he said: 'Well, girls, let's call it a day. I'm exhausted and asphyxiated and urgently in need of sustenance.'

'Shall I make some tea?' I asked.

'No, in return for treating me to a magnificent lunch I shall treat you to a humble supper. Go and scrape the paint off your faces and we'll away.'

I finished the last little patch of door and then stood up and surveyed the room. It really did look nice, all clean and white and sparkling and I suddenly saw flowery curtains at the window, in green and blue and white, and a blue carpet and divan cover. Tomorrow I'd paint the wooden chair white too, and when my books arrived I'd arrange them in the shelves in the alcove and put my ornaments on the mantelpiece.

We walked down the horrible stairs and up the horrible steps and then down the street they call the Royal Mile because it leads from the Castle to Holyrood Palace. There were funny little passages leading off the street called names like 'Advocates Close' or 'Riddles Court', mostly full of dustbins and boarded-up doors secured with barbed wire, but through some you could see right down to Princes Street and then to the sea. Mr McTaggart stopped to show me where Robert Burns had stayed and where a philosopher called David Hume had lived, and one big court where there was an old stone turreted house that used to belong to someone called Lady Stair and was now a museum.

Aunt Patsy became impatient.

'I thought you said you were hungry, Stephen. Emma has bags of time to rootle about and discover who lived where and why. I'm starving.'

So was I, though I was interested in what Mr McTaggart was telling me. What I couldn't understand was why, if this was the Royal Mile, it should be allowed to get into such a frightful mess. Lots of the windows were broken or boarded up and I actually saw grass growing in one of the gutters. When I asked, Mr McTaggart snorted and said:

'Have you no feeling for history?'

'History's all right but no one wants to live in a ruin,' I said sharply.

'You've got a point. If only stupid local authorities wouldn't let places fall to pieces before they realize their historical and architectural importance.

'Still, some renovations have been done. I'll show you Whitehorse Close, some time. It looks as if it was an illustration for Grimms' Fairy Tales.'

'Food,' said Aunt Patsy.

So we went into a little restaurant and ate spaghetti and fruit salad with ice cream.

*   *   *

The next few days I was so busy I didn't have time to feel homesick. We found the curtain material and I machined the curtains myself – they weren't exactly the same length but Aunt Patsy said it didn't matter. And we shopped for school clothes and in between I did mounds of washing-up because Aunt Patsy always forgot. She said there were two types of people, those who washed up after meals and those who washed up before, and she was the second sort. I didn't think I would ever get used to her ways. She was the most disorganized person I had ever met.

To start with, about meal-times. 'Aren't we going to have lunch?' I would say, and she would reply: 'Oh dear, are you hungry again? We'd better scramble some eggs,' as if it was unnatural and incomprehensible for me to be hungry at one o'clock.

Sometimes we had nothing but bread and cheese for supper and at other times she would say, 'I feel like a feast,' and spend hours in the kitchen making some complicated dish with rice and prawns and mushrooms and green peppers, followed by chocolate soufflé with whipped cream; and there would be wine for her and ginger beer for me, though she always said I could have wine if I wanted.

She was always running out of quite ordinary things like salt or coffee or butter and I would have to dash out and buy some at the last minute.

Luckily for her there was a little shop which seemed to be always open, even on Sundays. After a bit I started checking the larder and the fridge every morning and telling Aunt Patsy what we needed.

She was also disorganized about money. I couldn't make out if she was rich or poor. Sometimes she'd come home with a new gramophone record or bunches of flowers and at other times she'd say: 'We can't send any laundry this week – we'll have to wait till my cheque arrives.' It took me a long time to broach the subject of pocket-money because she must have had to spend pounds on my room and my uniform. But all the same a girl does need the odd shilling for sweets or paper hankies or pencils. I spent about a pound of my savings before I nerved myself to ask her.

'You should have told me,' she said crossly. 'How much do you want?'

'Mother used to give me five shillings every Saturday.'

'Well, here's a pound and tell me when you need some more.'

'I don't want a pound. I want five shillings every week. Otherwise I can't plan.'

'Do you have to be so methodical?' she burst out, and then stopped and smiled. 'All right, you shall have five shillings every Saturday.'

But of course she forgot and sometimes when I reminded her she hadn't got any money and then

I would have to remind her again. It was awful!

I discovered after a time that she was what you call a free-lance which meant she didn't get paid regularly, only when one of her illustrations or designs was accepted. But at first I couldn't understand why she didn't have a pay-day like other people. At home Father had always handed Mother the housekeeping every month when he got his salary cheque and she used to put so much aside for things like shoes and winter coats. But when a cheque did arrive Aunt Patsy would say: 'Goodie, goodie, let's go on the spree. What would you like? A new jersey or some roller skates or something for your room?' And how could I say what I wanted when I thought I might get left without a mackintosh or stockings?

We didn't exactly quarrel because during those first few weeks together we were both on our best behaviour. I was conscious how kind she was to look after me so that I didn't have to go to a horrible Home, and she was conscious that I was an orphan and needed to be cherished. Whenever she noticed that I was bored or unhappy she would ask me politely what I would like to do, go to a cinema or visit the Art Gallery or something like that. And I'd mutter she needn't bother and go and lie on my bed and think how much I hated Edinburgh, or write long letters to Richard explaining just how impossible Aunt Patsy was.

Richard wrote back long letters too and told

me what life with Aunt Laura was like.

'It appears that we have chosen the wrong aunts,' he wrote. 'You like being organized, so you would fit into Aunt Laura's house like a glove. We have meals on the dot and the same meals every week: roast beef on Sunday, cottage pie on Monday, sausages on Tuesday, and so on. And she asks Colin and me before every meal if we have washed our hands. And every evening at half past nine she says, "Well, boys, time for bed." She always says "boys", never our names. She talks about "boys" all the time – boys are always hungry, boys make too much noise, boys are untidy, boys like football. She doesn't think it's at all boyish when I want to play the piano or go for walks by myself. Colin is just as horrible as I remember. He's always wanting to wrestle and talks about football all the time and knows the name of every single player in every single team, and he won't learn to play chess. Uncle Edward plays with me sometimes but he does pretty well what Aunt Laura says because he is a "boy" too.

'The nice thing is that there is a really good music master at school, and he's going to teach me composition and harmony and all that jazz out of school hours. He says if I work hard I might get a scholarship to the Academy but I must practise three hours a day and with Aunt Laura sniffing and looking down her nose it's very difficult. She says I may practise an hour before breakfast and another hour between tea and supper but she's always finding reasons why it's inconvenient. And the piano is lousy.

'Still, I'm keeping a stiff upper lip. "Boys" always do! Shall I try and wangle you an invitation for Christmas? Or shall I come to Edinburgh?'

It seemed a marvellous idea, being with Richard and having meals on time and living in an organized household. If only Aunt Laura could have taken us both. You see, Richard is very different from me. He's always been terrifically independent and he likes being alone with his music or looking things up in encyclopaedias; he doesn't need people so much as things. And I don't mean he's one of those sissie boys – he's a super swimmer and he was in the tennis team at his old school and one of his ambitions is to be a rock climber. But he's never been like those boys who are always rolling on the grass wrestling or kicking balls about or making extraordinary noises like tractors or machine guns. It really was a pity we had got the wrong aunts because I could see quite clearly that Richard wouldn't be annoyed by Aunt Patsy at all. She'd be at her drawing board making squiggles and he'd be at the piano playing scales and when they were hungry they'd eat and when they were tired they'd go to bed without bothering about the time at all.

And I wouldn't mind being called 'girls' by Aunt

Laura or being asked if I'd wash my hands or told when it was bedtime. I don't think Aunt Patsy would have noticed or cared if I stayed up till midnight. At first I used to look at the clock around half past nine and wonder if she would say: 'Time for bed, Emma!' But she never did. I used to yawn and fidget and then say: 'Don't you think it's time I went to bed?'

'If you want. No one's stopping you.'

I couldn't help missing the way Mother used to get my milk and biscuits, and say she'd be up in half an hour to turn my light off, and kiss me goodnight. Sometimes she'd just kiss me and tell me to sleep well, and at other times she'd sit on my bed and we'd have a cosy chat about school or what colour I'd like my winter coat or things that happened to her when she was a little girl. It made me feel very lonely and cut off to choose my own bedtime and turn off my own light.

If only I could persuade Aunt Laura that I was the sort of girl she'd like and persuade Aunt Patsy that Richard was the sort of boy she'd like, without being rude or ungrateful!

Chapter Five

I WAS dreading my first day at school. New schools of any sort are bad enough. I hated it when I started Grammar School in London and had to get used to new teachers and different rules. It's partly because I'm what Mother used to call 'a creature of habit' and partly because although I'm not shy at meeting one or two strange people, a lot of strangers make me feel terribly tongue-tied and stupid.

But after all in London I already had several friends and I did start at the beginning of the term. Also I had Mother to boost my morale when I got home and Father to help me with my Latin and Geometry homework.

Starting school in Edinburgh was going to be sheer murder, I thought gloomily. The term had already started and everyone would know I was an orphan and feel sorry for me. And everything would probably be taught differently in some stupid Scottish way, and instead of being near the top of the class, I'd probably be the prize dunce.

Aunt Patsy had rung up the Education Committee and fixed for me to go to what is called a

Senior Secondary School. (They don't appear to have Grammar Schools in Edinburgh.) It was called Parkhill.

'All schools are pretty awful in my opinion,' said Aunt Patsy. 'I know I never learnt a thing but it's the law. So there's nothing we can do about it.'

'But you have to be educated,' I said, rather horrified.

'Education!' Aunt Patsy sniffed. 'What have square roots, and the date of the Battle of Trafalgar, and being able to translate some Roman general's reminiscences into pidgin English to do with education? I'd throw children into public libraries and art galleries and see what happened.'

'But then we'd never pass our exams.'

'Quite!' said Aunt Patsy.

I found out later that she had left school at fifteen and done all sorts of horrible jobs like working in a bakery and serving in a shop until she won a scholarship to Art School.

'If I don't get "A" level in at least three subjects,' I said, 'I'll never find an interesting job.'

'I did,' said Aunt Patsy.

I was just going to say, 'But that was in the olden days,' then I thought it would be rude so I said instead: 'It's different if you're an artist.'

Anyhow to school I had to go, and we bought an alarm clock and Aunt Patsy, rather unwillingly, agreed to go with me. 'It gives me the shudders just going into a school,' she said, 'and as for being smarmy to headmasters . . .'

I wanted to say, 'All right, if that's the way you feel I'll go alone,' but I couldn't bring myself to. I just hoped and prayed she wouldn't wear her

slacks and look too eccentric. However, she wore her green corduroy suit and actually looked rather smart.

'And you will be here when I get back?' I asked.

'I daresay.'

Parkhill is in what they call the New Town because it is only about a hundred years old! It's

44

quite different from the Old Town, and has squares and gardens and terraces built in circles called circuses and crescents, rather like some parts of London. And a lot of the buildings have pillars and funny bits of statuary. I liked it because of the trees and the gardens, and because the houses didn't look as though they would fall down any minute, the way they did in the Old Town.

Naturally the school wasn't new. It looked rather like my idea of a prison or a reformatory – a great square high building in sooty stone surrounded by a concrete playground with high spiky railings. The date over the door was 1899. Probably, I thought, it's still lit by gas and we have to write on slates.

'Aren't there any new schools?' I asked Aunt Patsy as we stepped off the bus.

'Oh yes,' said Aunt Patsy. 'In the suburbs they've built several, all glass and concrete and bright coloured tiles. I must say, this does look rather awful. But never mind. It's supposed to be quite a good school – as schools go.'

To be honest, it wasn't quite as bad inside as I had feared. It was light and the paintwork was pale blue and it didn't remind me of a prison at all.

But something else struck me.

'Do you mean there are boys too?' I asked.

'Of course. Nearly all Scottish schools are co-educational. Didn't you know?'

45

I gulped. It had just never occurred to me. I'd heard people discussing coeducation, and Mother had always said it was a bad thing because boys and girls developed at different speeds and were good at different things.

The place seemed suddenly full of boys – great

tall, practically grown-up boys, and middle-sized pimply boys with weird hair styles, and little midgetty boys staggering under the weight of enormous school bags, all looking exactly like what Aunt Laura meant when she said 'boys'.

I followed Aunt Patsy up the stairs to the head-master's room feeling worse and worse.

The headmaster was small and fat and grey with an india-rubbery face and a toothy smile. He shook both our hands.

'Ah, Miss Grieve,' he said, 'and this is Emma.'

As I obviously was Emma there didn't seem anything to reply. So I sort of smirked.

'I'm afraid it will all seem rather strange at first,' he said to me, 'but I'm sure you'll settle down soon.'

Again I gave a tepid smile.

'You've been doing Latin and French, haven't you, so I've put you into Miss Morrison's class, number five, and we'll see how you get on. I'll just get one of the prefects to take you to your class-room, that is unless there's anything you would like to ask me.'

I did want to ask him something frightfully badly, but it was difficult.

'Please, could you not tell anyone about' – I gulped – 'my parents.'

'Of course not, my dear child. Now,' he picked up his telephone, pressed a knob, and said:

'Miss Vaughan, would you find one of the pre-fects and ask her to take Emma to Miss Morrison's class, please.' A minute later there was a knock on the door. I shook hands with the headmaster again, Aunt Patsy gave me a rueful look as if to say, 'I told you schools were awful and head-masters fools but what can we do?' and I followed a very tall snooty-looking girl down the stairs again.

The classroom was on the ground floor but the windows were too high up to look out of. The desks were all double ones but I was relieved to find that the boys sat on one side of the room and the girls on the other. Miss Morrison, our class teacher, was youngish and quite pretty, and gave me a smile. She wrote my name down, handed me hundreds of books and exercise books (they call them jotters) and introduced me to the class: 'This is Emma Langham, and she's from London, so I hope you'll all help her to find her way about.'

The girl she put me to sit beside was called Elizabeth Cameron. She had shoulder-length mouse-coloured hair in such a very long fringe I couldn't see much of her face but what I could see seemed nice. All the same it was horrible to have to sit so close to a perfect stranger – no privacy at all.

'Have you come to stay here?' she whispered.

'No, I'm just on a visit,' I whispered back.

'Is your father in the Army?'

'No. He's an engineer. My mother's in hospital so I'm staying with an aunt.'

'How long for?'

'I don't know. Probably till Christmas.'

I don't approve of lies but you can't go round telling people that you're a very new orphan because they just get embarrassed and don't know what to say. I remember a girl at my other school whose mother died and of course we all wanted to be specially nice to her but we didn't know how.

The first lesson was Maths and we were given a perfectly easy problem but for some reason I couldn't concentrate. Ordinarily I'm pretty good at Maths.

After a few minutes Elizabeth Cameron nudged my elbow and pushed a piece of paper on to my desk with the answer written on it. I was furious. As if I wanted any help! I scrumpled it up and dropped it on the floor and shook my head violently.

'Sorry I'm sure,' she whispered in a huffy voice.

Then the Maths teacher, who was red-faced and bald and called Mr Hamilton, did the problem on the board and asked whoever had it right to put up their hands.

'And you-er-Emma,' he said, 'are you familiar with this type of problem?'

I blushed and nodded. I daresay he was trying to be helpful but it's beastly to be picked on on your very first day.

At break we all went into the horrible concrete

playground and most of the girls said Hello to me, and asked me the same questions, and I elaborated a bit, and told them my mother had rheumatic fever but they'd just discovered some absolutely super new drug so that she'd be well again in no time. And I'm afraid I boasted that Aunt Patsy was a famous artist who lived in a historic house near the Castle that had been in the family for generations, and that my school in London was the very latest design. (Actually it was quite old too.) Once you start lying it's difficult to stop. I saw how I'd like everything to be and I couldn't resist the chance to make it that way even though, at the same time, I knew it was stupid.

After a bit the girls became bored and started talking about who was gone on who, and wasn't the Maths teacher a beast to have given us so much homework, and other school gossip, and as it was all about people I had never heard of I got bored too and drifted away. Then the bell rang.

We had History next which was confusing, because it was the history of Scotland, and the only things I knew were about Mary, Queen of Scots being beheaded, and Robert Bruce winning the Battle of Bannockburn. But the History teacher was nice and made it all as interesting as possible.

The Latin teacher was a little bright-eyed old lady with white hair and a pink face who seemed to think Latin was so dull she must cheer it up by telling us lots of jokes and describing her holidays in Italy where her knowledge of Latin 'had been so useful'. I had a suspicion that the class had heard her jokes before but they all laughed politely. And I couldn't help thinking, too, that Italian would have been a great deal more useful than Latin for a holiday in Italy.

Elizabeth Cameron didn't try to help me again and I put a stack of books at my side of the desk so she couldn't see what I was writing.

Dinner was the worst part of the day because the dining-room was so crowded we all had our elbows practically in each other's plates, and the mince was gristly, and the custard too sweet, and the sponge was full of dates that tasted like penicillin tablets. But then, in my experience, school dinners always are vile.

I felt very tired when eventually the bell rang at a quarter to four and I filled Aunt Patsy's old music case, which she had lent me, with all the books I had been given. It weighed a ton and I didn't look forward to lugging it up the hill.

'Do we have to take all our books home?' I asked Elizabeth.

'Of course.'

'What a bind!'

At the bus stop there was a great jostling queue and the bigger boys simply smashed their way through it. A girl who was standing beside me gave one of them a smart kick on the ankle and darted on to the bus while he looked round. Fortunately there weren't so many people for my bus so I didn't have to resort to such drastic tactics.

Still I was pretty exhausted when I finally staggered up the stairs and let myself into the flat.

'Yoohoo,' I called, which was what I always did at home when I got back from school.

There was no reply. The kitchen was empty, except for the usual pile of washing-up, and the studio was empty except for the usual trail of coffee cups and bulging ashtrays. Aunt Patsy was out.

Mother was always home at four o'clock and she always had tea ready, and suddenly I felt utterly miserable. I sat down at the kitchen table and cried. Horrible Edinburgh! Horrible school! And horrible Aunt Patsy.

Then I pulled myself together, filled the kettle and lit the gas and laid the table for two – surely Aunt Patsy would be back soon. I tackled the washing-up while the kettle was boiling. Then I made the tea and toasted two bits of bread. Still no Aunt Patsy. I leaned out of the window but apart from the usual silly tourists coming to look at the

Castle there was nobody. So I ate my tea by myself.

Aunt Patsy didn't get home till six o'clock. I heard her call 'Emma!' but I was lying on my bed and I didn't reply. I was too angry with her. She knocked on my door and came in.

'Hullo. How are you? How was school?'

'You weren't in,' I said accusingly. 'I made tea and everything and you didn't come.'

'Emma, I'm sorry, I just had to go and see someone about a job.'

'I bet you forgot,' I mumbled.

'I didn't forget. I just couldn't make it.'

'You don't care.'

Aunt Patsy went pink. I thought for a moment she was going to be angry and tell me I was a bore and a nuisance and I could jolly well go into a Home for all she cared. Instead she tightened her mouth and looked out of the window. In a way I wanted her to be angry but she just spoke very quietly.

'Look, Emma, I have to earn my living and if a chance of a job comes up I simply have to take it. Sometimes I'll be in and sometimes I won't and you'll have to put up with it. You're quite old enough to be reasonable.'

The trouble was I didn't feel at all old enough to be reasonable. So I went on lying on my bed feeling sorry for myself until Aunt Patsy told me supper was ready. We were very polite at supper

53

about passing the butter and the salt, and we didn't talk. After supper she went up to the studio and I went back into my room and did my homework.

Chapter Six

I DON'T know exactly when it was that I stopped
hating everything so much. It was like when
you've been ill in bed for a long time and you wake
up one morning and think 'I'm well' and you
actually feel hungry for breakfast. Mother used to
give me, on these occasions, a lightly boiled egg
and brown bread and butter cut very thin and I
used to eat it very slowly because it tasted so delicious. And then I'd get up and go into the garden
and everything would look and smell clean and
new, especially the sycamore tree.

Something like this happened to me now. I
woke up one morning and thought, goodie, History today, and I shot out of bed and looked out of
the window and suddenly realized I liked looking
at all the slatey-blue roofs and chimney-pots and
the green hill they call Arthur's Seat. And I liked
hearing the milkman's horse clop-clopping up the
hill and the chink of bottles and the scruffy-
looking starling that sat making wolf-whistles on
the gutter.

As I got washed and dressed I felt conscious of
the beautiful way all the bits of my body were

joined together and I thought how clever my muscles were to do so quickly what I wanted them to do. And I smiled at myself in the mirror as if I were being introduced to someone who would say, Who is that beautiful and talented girl?

I decided to make bacon and eggs for breakfast and I put Aunt Patsy's on a tray and knocked at her door and said, 'Surprise,' just like my father used to say when he did it for me or Mother.

Aunt Patsy blinked and mumbled something but I just drew her curtains and brought up a chair to put the tray on.

'Emma,' she protested. 'What on earth's got into you?'

'It's a marvellous morning,' I said. 'You can't waste it asleep.'

I discovered later that she loathed breakfast in bed and that bacon and eggs first thing in the morning gave her indigestion but she put on a very convincing act of thanking me and saying she felt like a duchess.

Recently, Aunt Patsy and I had been awfully polite to one another without ever really saying anything. She had made a great effort to be in at four o'clock and had almost resigned herself to doing the washing-up after instead of before meals. She always asked me how I had got on at school and I always asked her if she had had a good day but we had just been strangers living in

the same house, certainly not friends or relations.

And I suddenly thought what a bind it must
have been for her to alter her whole life for someone I could hardly believe she even liked.

So after breakfast I went back into her room
and said: 'You don't have to be in for tea. I don't
really mind.'

She grinned, though she was still rather sleepy
and hadn't made much headway with her breakfast. Then she said: 'Let's have something nice for
supper. What would you like? I might ask
Stephen and make it a party.'

'Can we have it all laid out properly with table
mats and butter knives?'

'Your word is my command.'

'And flowers?'

'Why not?'

'I mean, can we afford it?'

'We can. I got a very good cheque this week.'

'Then let's have roast pork and apple sauce and
trifle with lots of cream.'

'Ugh, I can't bear to think of food at this time of
the morning.'

'Well, you asked me.'

'So I did.'

'And can we have salted nuts and cheesey biscuits to nibble while we're waiting?'

'Ugh,' said Aunt Patsy again and shut her
eyes.

I don't mean from all this that I had given up my plan of exchanging Aunt Patsy for Aunt Laura. I knew that Aunt Patsy and I just weren't suited. But I also knew that she was being as nice to me as she could and probably a great deal nicer than I deserved. And I knew that Mother would strongly disapprove if I went on sulking and narking. It suddenly seemed very easy not to sulk and nark. After all it would only be until Christmas.

I met the postman on the stairs – and don't think I had suddenly decided to like *them* – and he gave me a letter from Richard which I read on the bus.

'All sorts of plots and plans are brewing,' he wrote. 'To start with the insurance money has come through which has cheered Aunt Laura up no end – I mean "boys" are so expensive, always growing out of their clothes, etc. It also appears that she has been appointed our guardian and so will be able to decide whether you are being properly looked after, or not, as you seem to think. She definitely disapproves of Aunt Patsy, with her nasty bohemian habits, irregular hours, unsuitable friends and so on. The money having arrived, she is now talking about sending me to boarding school and going to Edinburgh to investigate the appallingly unsuitable conditions she is sure you are living in, ha ha! I think if she finds that you are a "nice" girl and liable to fit into a "nice" home she might consider taking you into "the bosom of". As for me, I am in disgrace for being so unboyish as to prefer music to football.

'At first I wasn't sure about the boarding school idea but, as you know, I am not such a home body as you and when I talked to Mr Chator (the music master) he said he thought I could get a scholarship to a really super school where music is taken seriously.

'I'm pretty sure that M-O-N-E-Y counts more with Aunt Laura than anything else so if she finds one of those schools that are all discipline and keeping a stiff upper lip and a healthy mind in a healthy body, I shall be able to make a counter-suggestion with a scholarship cheque clutched in my unboyish hand.

'Is Edinburgh really so awful? Are you sure it's Aunt Patsy and not just you? Think twice, dear sister, before you exchange your crumbling bohemian attic for a nice suitable home.'

This was a terribly exciting letter. I thought Richard was being just too stupid about Aunt Laura. Of course money was important. It was important to Aunt Patsy too; perhaps with the insurance money she'd be able to buy the blue carpet she'd promised me.

Then I remembered that by Christmas I'd be living in Exeter, Richard would be back for the holidays and life would be marvellous. It would be nice, too, for Aunt Patsy who must be bored to death with my fussing about the washing-up and having meals on time.

School started off well. I even smiled at Elizabeth Cameron and didn't put a pile of books between her desk and mine, and I was top of the History test.

Now I want to make it clear before I describe what happened next that the teachers at Parkhill were, as teachers go, all reasonably nice. They had their quirks and oddities of course but in general, if you behaved adequately, they treated you as a human being. There are days when even the nicest teacher obviously has a headache or indigestion or the beginning of flu and then if anyone plays up they tend to go mad. And in any class there are always one or two pupils, especially boys, who aren't interested and who do everything they can to get a rise out of a teacher. They ask silly questions and drop things and talk and throw india-rubbers at each other. And they don't apparently mind being caned, or getting the belt as it's called in Scotland.

But Mr Hamilton, the Maths teacher, seemed to suffer from permanent headaches (or indigestion or flu) because he was always in a bad temper. His big red face used to go even redder and he would shout and bang his hand on the desk and wave his belt around like a cowboy with a lassoo. Even when he wasn't angry he always spoke in that nasty sarcastic way: 'I wonder if I could trouble you to rise from your seat and approach the blackboard,' or 'It appears that our mathematical genius in the back row is under the impression that two and two make five,' which we all hated.

I used to do quite well in Maths but it was more to spite him than to please him. I liked to do a problem very quickly and then, as if bored, sit looking at the ceiling. When he thought he had me napping and asked if I could bear just giving him a quarter of my attention, I would give the right answer in a superior voice.

I knew he was dying to catch me out and I was determined that he shouldn't. One day I even found a mistake in one of his calculations. Delighted I put up my hand. 'Excuse me, sir, but I don't understand.'

'You don't understand? I thought that with your experience in the southern part of the island there was little we poor Scots could do to puzzle your superior knowledge.'

'The figure on the right,' I said. 'I don't understand why it's 59 and not 58.'

'What? What?' he barked. 'Oh I see. Yes, yes.'

He scowled at me and I looked as innocent as possible and one of the boys tittered but as he was looking at me he didn't see which one. So he gave us all extra homework to relieve his feelings.

This particular morning he was even worse

than usual. Perhaps he had quarrelled with his wife because she had burnt the toast or he had left his umbrella on the bus.

He stormed into the classroom, gave us all a row for not standing up fast enough and told us we were the laziest set of nincompoops he had ever had the misfortune to teach. He was going to give us a test and anyone who got less than ten out of twenty would be given double homework.

'And anyone who gets less than five,' he snarled, taking out his belt and giving it a swish, 'will make closer acquaintance with Oscar here.' (He always called the belt 'Oscar' – stupid!)

One or two people snickered nervously and then we all bent over the test. Even though I knew I wasn't likely to get less than ten I couldn't help feeling nervous and my heart beat in the way that makes you feel everyone must be able to hear it.

Elizabeth, beside me, was even more nervous. I could hear her giving little sighs of desperation and she kept licking her lips.

When I was nearly through I looked round and caught her eye and gave her an encouraging smile. She shook her head and turned her eyes towards the ceiling. I glanced at her paper and saw that she had only got as far as number four.

Although we often help each other with our homework or ordinary classwork it's understood that when we do tests it's each man for himself.

Still, every rule has its exception and I felt this certainly was cause for one.

I tilted my papers sideways so that Elizabeth could see at least some of my answers, but she was hunched over her desk and didn't look up. I gave her a tiny kick on the ankle and nodded as if to say, 'It's all right, go ahead.' Then I became very absorbed in the next question and didn't dare to see if Elizabeth was taking advantage of my help or not.

'Elizabeth Cameron!' boomed out the voice of Mr Hamilton.

'Y-yes, sir,' she stammered.

'When I give tests I expect the results to be the unaided efforts of your own brain, however woefully inadequate that organ is, not the joint efforts of you and the distinguished scholar on your left.'

'Yes, sir,' said poor Elizabeth.

Her face was always half-hidden behind her hair but the bit of it I could see was crimson.

'Oscar would like a few words with you, Elizabeth.'

Elizabeth stumbled up to his desk and held out her hand. I was so furious I didn't care that I was playing right into Mr Hamilton's hands.

'It's unfair!' I shouted.

Mr Hamilton glared at me.

'Oh?' he drawled.

'It was my fault. I wanted to help her.'

'I don't know what the custom is in the southern part of the island,' he sneered, 'but in Scotland cheating is regarded as dishonourable.'

I knew it was crazy to answer a teacher back (any teacher) but I couldn't stop, in spite of Mr Hamilton looking apoplectic and running his belt through his fingers. Although red-haired people are supposed to have hot tempers I don't often lose mine; but when I do it's like a galloping horse.

'Helping isn't cheating,' I burst out.

'Really? How interesting! How informative!'

'And in any case,' I went on in a rush, 'she could have done the test perfectly well if you hadn't made her so nervous.'

'So the age of chivalry is not dead,' drawled Mr Hamilton. 'If you wish to suffer alongside your friend, who am I to stand in your way? Approach the desk, please.'

So I walked up and stood beside Elizabeth and he hit us both with his beastly belt. It was horrible. No one had ever hit me before in my life. I don't mean I'm always angelically well-behaved. From time to time I've been sent to bed early or had my pocket-money docked or just been given a talking to. But hit – never. I didn't know I could feel so angry.

Elizabeth was crying when we went back to our desks but I wasn't. I was just seething with fury. I stuffed my books angrily into my school bag and stumped straight out of the classroom, giving Mr

Hamilton what I hoped was a withering look.

Just as I reached the main hall the bell rang for the dinner break but I didn't go into the dining-hall. I went out of the door and across the playground and out into the street. The lollipop man in his white coat was standing by the bus stop for the primary children who mostly went home to dinner.

'Going home early?' he asked. He was a nice cheery man.

'I'm not feeling well,' I said and let him stop the traffic for me to go across the road to my bus stop on the other side.

'You don't look so good and that's a fact,' he said sympathetically. 'There's a lot of flu going round.'

It's funny that whenever you have a cold or a sore throat someone always tells you that there's a lot of it going around.

All the way home in the bus I kept saying to myself, 'I'll never go there again. The beast, the absolute beast.'

I simply raced up the stairs and rushed into the flat. Aunt Patsy was sitting in the kitchen drinking coffee and reading the paper and before I had thought what I was going to do or say I had flung my arms round her and burst into tears.

Aunt Patsy was utterly bewildered but she held me tightly and kept saying: 'What happened, Emma? What's the matter, darling?'

66

I choked and sobbed and then I blew my nose and sat down beside her and told her the whole story. At the back of my mind I realized that she had never called me Darling before.

She was just as angry as I had been. She kept exclaiming, 'Disgusting! Revolting behaviour! What a swine!' and she lit cigarettes and stamped round the room and said that I need never go to school again, that all the School Inspectors in the world wouldn't force her to send me, that she'd go to jail first, and other comforting things.

'The spectacle of a grown man beating little girls makes me spew,' she spluttered. 'Now don't worry, Emma, there's no headmaster in the world who can frighten me.'

When I had calmed down she wanted me to have some lunch but I felt I'd be sick, so I just had a cup of tea and a piece of toast and Marmite. And then Aunt Patsy strode to the telephone as if she were going to impale it on a bayonet, dialled the number with savage little jabs of her finger and asked to speak to the headmaster.

I felt rather cosy and exhausted sitting in the kitchen listening to Aunt Patsy's voice.

'I hear from my niece that she has been attacked by one of the vile sadistic thugs you employ to instruct her in Mathematics ... Either you sack him immediately or I shall go to the Education Committee and raise Cain ... It's abominable that grown men are allowed to hit little girls under your revolting system of so-called education . . . I shall take him to court and charge him with assault . . . I won't allow my niece to set foot in your deplorable school again . . .'

Then she came back into the kitchen looking smug.

'I've scared him out of his wits,' she said with a chuckle. 'He wants me to go to the school this afternoon and tell him exactly what happened and then he will "take steps". He is deeply apologetic, ha ha! Didn't you think I was impressive on the phone, Emma?'

'You were marvellous. I don't suppose anyone's ever spoken to him like that before in his life.'

'I don't suppose so. And it's high time someone did. Now Emma, why don't you lie on your bed with a book and when I come back with his head on a spear we'll have tea together. And after that we'll cook our delicious celebration supper.'

Chapter Seven

SUPPER that evening was a great success. I
cleared the table in the studio and laid it with
matching cutlery and plates – Aunt Patsy did have
nice things, she was just too lazy to use them half
the time. We arranged some lovely white chry-
santhemums in a red jug and polished the fur-
niture, and the whole room looked quite civilized
for once.

Aunt Patsy had made the trifle and put it in the
fridge but she had allowed me to decorate it with
whipped cream and cherries and chopped nuts. I
also arranged the before-supper drinks on a tray
with the salted nuts and potato crisps and cheesey
biscuits in little bowls.

So when Stephen McTaggart arrived everything
was ready, both Aunt Patsy and I were clean and
brushed, wearing nylons without snags in them,
and the new corduroy pinafores we had just
bought: Aunt Patsy's was pale blue and mine was
honey colour.

She had come back from her interview with the
headmaster in high spirits but she just said: 'I'll
tell you about it at supper. It's so boring to have to

tell a story twice. Everything's going to be all right.'

So I felt rather gay too and to my surprise I quite enjoyed telling Stephen what had happened at school and imitating Mr Hamilton; in fact I even made them both laugh. It's peculiar that things which make you furious or upset at the time can make you laugh when you tell them afterwards.

Then Aunt Patsy told Stephen about her telephone conversation and she made us laugh too. So when she came to describing her interview we were all quite giggly.

I don't know exactly what she said to the headmaster because often when you tell a story you slightly improve what you said and what he said, but apparently he had been very nice and understanding. He said he had been trying to get a replacement for Mr Hamilton for some time as he had not been satisfied with his teaching methods, but that there was a terrific shortage of teachers. He'd go immediately to the Education Department and insist on a replacement but he'd be hardly likely to get one until next term.

Aunt Patsy said in that case she'd keep me at home for the rest of the term and if anyone asked why, she'd jolly well tell them.

The headmaster gave his personal assurance that Mr Hamilton wouldn't lay a finger on me again. What about the other girls? Aunt Patsy had asked. She didn't want anyone to be beaten. A man who threatened defenceless children with physical violence wasn't fit to be entrusted with teaching them.

Well, the headmaster said, he quite understood but there were limits of his powers of interference. The whole question of corporal punishment was under review and many teachers were against it nowadays; he personally was in favour of restricting it to really serious offences but, because of the shortage of teachers, overcrowded classes and so on and so forth . . .

Aunt Patsy snorted: she hadn't yet given up the idea of reporting the whole matter to the Director of Education, charging Mr Hamilton with assault, and giving the story to the press.

The headmaster promised he would look into the whole matter immediately and let her know within the next few days. But he did feel it would be a mistake to deprive a promising scholar of half a term's work. It might seriously prejudice my chances in the exams.

So then Aunt Patsy told him exactly what she thought about exams. I wish I had been there.

'So here you are and here you stay,' said Aunt Patsy triumphantly, 'until that monster has been removed.'

While we had been unfolding our tale Stephen had been chuckling and saying, 'Good for you,' and 'You're absolutely right,' and 'The thug,' and things of that sort. But when she had finished he stared at Aunt Patsy in quite a different way and said: 'Patsy, you're marvellous!'

Until now I hadn't noticed anybody or anything except as they'd appeared to me. I suppose I had been completely self-centred. But now I looked at Stephen and Aunt Patsy in quite a different way, looking at them both as they must appear to each other.

Aunt Patsy, sitting on a tufftie by the electric fire, in her nice blue corduroy pinafore that made her eyes look blue too, was flushed and almost pretty. And although you couldn't call Stephen handsome he did look distinguished and interesting as he sat on the sofa and leaned forward to touch her hand when he told her she was marvellous. He always wore dark green or dark blue shirts with peculiar ties or polo-necked sweaters and his donkey jacket was a disgrace. His teeth weren't good and he had a round bald patch on the top of his head. But his light-blue eyes had a sort of electric sharpness and there were little lines on his face that made him look kind, and his smile always seemed as though he were really smiling, not just being polite.

I decided they must like each other very much indeed and that I liked them both very much too. So I got up and went downstairs to make coffee. Of course I hadn't the faintest intention of staying away from school. That would have been stupid because I knew the value of exams even if Aunt Patsy didn't. I wasn't really frightened of Mr Hamilton and now that I had recovered and been made a fuss of and eaten a delicious meal (the trifle was fabulous) I was even looking forward to going back to school and having a good gossip with everyone. So I hummed happily to myself as I made coffee and put Aunt Patsy's best coffee service on a tray. (I discovered it at the back of a cupboard where she had forgotten it.)

Perhaps Stephen had seen a completely 'new side' to Aunt Patsy and now he would fall in love with her. Then she'd have someone to pay the laundry bills and she could move into a civilized new house with a garden, and perhaps (I'm a bit ashamed of thinking this) I'd even have my blue carpet.

When I returned to the studio with the coffee they were both sitting on the sofa which I thought was an encouraging sign.

'What did we ever do without Emma?' Stephen said smiling. 'Butter plates and paper napkins and coffee in the best cups! What a transformation! What a reformation!'

Aunt Patsy and I looked at each other and for a moment I thought *she* looked annoyed and that *I* felt annoyed, but then we both laughed.

'Soon I'll be wearing gloves and a hat,' Aunt Patsy said.

'Never!' said Stephen.

'Sipping tea, with my little finger curled up, with all the best Edinburgh ladies,' continued Aunt Patsy simpering.

'Learning to play bridge and writing letters to the papers about the Decline of Modern Youth.'

'Please, no!'

'The people in Castlehill will set their watches by me because of the punctuality with which I dispatch my duties and when I die they'll put on my gravestone: "By her sobriety, godliness and righteousness she set an example to the people of this parish".'

'Promise,' said Stephen to me, 'that you won't reform Patsy too much.'

I smiled rather smugly. It was intoxicating to think of reforming anyone, even a little, let alone too much. Privately I thought I had made very little headway and that if Aunt Patsy wanted to get married, to Stephen, for instance, she still had a long way to go before she would make him a suitable wife.

At that moment the door bell rang and Stephen said: 'Oh, by the way, as you felt like a party, I asked some of my students to drop in.' (Stephen taught part-time at the Art College.)

I felt a bit disappointed because we were having such a cosy time, just the three of us, but I went down to open the door and four or five people burst in, carrying guitars and tins of Coca-Cola and beer, all laughing and talking. They were a pretty weird lot, mostly wearing jeans and jerseys which could have done with a wash, and with hair badly in need of cutting. They all had names like Lil or Bett or Jim or Dave and I could never remember which was which. (Some of them had visited us before but I usually went to my room to get out of the way.)

This time they all became very excited looking at some new designs of Aunt Patsy's. They made me quite ashamed that I'd never really found out what she was doing when she sat up late at night at her drawing-board. Apparently one of those boutique shops had asked her to design some tiles and one of the students, Jim (or Dave), was going to fire them for her.

I looked at the designs and really they were rather nice. There were some in splodgy blues and greens with butterfly shapes and some in splodgy oranges and browns in flower shapes.

While the others were admiring them I fetched more glasses and a beer-can opener and rescued the precious coffee cups from possible accidents. By the time I had returned, one of the girls was playing the piano. Then Dave tuned his guitar and sang some folk songs, and soon everyone was talking and drinking and joining in the songs, and talking and drinking again. I did not talk much because they were all a lot older than me and I don't know anything about art. I just filled their

glasses and passed ashtrays so they wouldn't drop ash on the floor.

It wasn't the sort of party I usually like but because of my special mood I found I was enjoying myself. We had drawn the curtains and the lamplight made shadows on the white walls; the piano, which we had polished till it shone, reflected the light; and the guitar made a nice twangy background noise.

In fact after all the excitement and the good food I felt rather as if my body had gone to sleep and that the rest of me was floating on some sort of cushiony cloud, so that I could think and notice with a special sharpness without being able to move or talk. I could see Aunt Patsy and Stephen sitting on the sofa talking earnestly together; and the students mostly on the floor, with glasses in their hands, jabbering away, except for the one called Jim who was bent over his guitar, and the one called Lil who was leaning against the mantelpiece singing a song about a lassie with a yellow coatie.

I don't know how long this mood lasted but quite by accident my eyes wandered to the clock on the mantelpiece. It was usually wrong but I had set it right before the party. And to my horror I found it was half past eleven, long past my bedtime. What would Mother have said, I suddenly thought with a pang: at home I'd only been allowed to stay up late on very special occasions like Christmas and my birthday and then certainly not later than half past ten. There wasn't a hope that Aunt Patsy would look up and say: 'Gracious, child, it's high time you were in bed!'

But then, I reflected, Aunt Patsy couldn't help it. She had never had a daughter and didn't know what mothers are expected to do, and after all she had shown that she had my interests at heart. So when she looked across at me and smiled and said, 'Enjoying yourself, Emma?' I just smiled back and went on floating on my cloud. After all it was Saturday tomorrow and we'd be able to have a late breakfast.

I didn't look at the clock again but presently everyone started getting ready to go home. They made a terrific noise galumphing down the stairs and I couldn't imagine what the neighbours would think; and then Aunt Patsy and I were left alone, yawning and blinking at each other.

'Let's leave the washing-up till tomorrow,' said Aunt Patsy coaxingly.

For a moment I was going to say No, we'll do it now; then I relented.

'Let's,' I said.

Chapter Eight

THE next morning Aunt Patsy and I got up rather late, about nine o'clock. We spent an hour clearing away and washing up after the party and then settled down to a quiet breakfast of boiled eggs and lots of toast and marmalade (for Aunt Patsy) and honey (for me) and tea (for Aunt Patsy) and Nescafé (for me). We were both rather sleepy so we didn't talk much but over our second cups Aunt Patsy said, 'Stephen and I are thinking it would be rather nice to get married. What do you think?'

'I think it would be super,' I said quickly. 'I mean he's awfully nice and you have got Art in common even though—' I choked back what I was going to say next.

'Even though what?'

'He's a bit bald,' I mumbled shamefacedly.

Aunt Patsy roared with laughter so I knew I hadn't hurt her feelings.

At that moment, just as I was going to ask all sorts of questions, the postman arrived with Aunt Laura's letter. Aunt Patsy read it with, every minute, her eyebrows going higher, her nose getting longer, and the corners of her mouth turning in a satirical way.

'Well, well, well!' she said. 'Laura has all sorts of ideas about your future – about all our futures, in fact.'

'Tell me,' I begged.

'I don't know' – began Aunt Patsy – 'but, oh well, it's your future so you ought to hear the letter itself, not just what I think of it.'

She began to read.

Dear Patsy,

The Will has appointed me as guardian to poor Richard and Emma and now the insurance money has come through it will be possible to do the sort of thing that Christine would have wished.

In the case of dear Richard I feel the answer is clearly a good boarding school. He has not really settled down to our way of life and cannot be said to have fitted in, though I have done my best for him. He is not a very cooperative boy.

As for Emma, I have no doubt that she has been somewhat an inconvenience to you, knowing the free-and-easy life you lead, and that you will be pleased to hear that it will now be possible to send her to a boarding school too.

On the other hand, from what I learned about her from Christine and the chance remarks of her brother, she seems essentially the sort of girl who would benefit from family life and, if I am satisfied that she would fit in, I would consider taking her under our roof and providing the sort of background for her that I am sure she would appreciate.

I realize that it was your keen sense of duty and family obligations that led you to give Emma a temporary home in Edinburgh but I am sure that you will be pleased to be freed of that obligation now that a suitable alternative offers itself.

As for myself, it is hardly necessary to tell you that I want the best for my dear nephew and niece.

I am coming up to Edinburgh in the near future when we can discuss the matter. Please do not offer to put me up as I know of your cramped surroundings and I would not dream of inconveniencing you.

Yours affectionately,
Laura

On hearing this letter I was filled with so many conflicting feelings I didn't know what to say.

First I felt Hooray! Aunt Laura will find out how nice I am and how unsuitably I am being looked after and she will take me back to Exeter, and I shall live in a nice family house in the country. On the other hand I realized I liked Aunt

Patsy and I liked living in Edinburgh, and I didn't want to go to a boarding school or stay in a house where I was just a 'girl'. I'd rather have had irregular meals and bedtimes and be treated as a person. Still, if Aunt Patsy was going to marry Stephen they wouldn't want to start off with a great lump of ready-made family (me); I mean people just don't, they like their own children but not other people's.

It all led to two conclusions: if I behaved nicely, Aunt Laura would whisk me off to Exeter; and if I behaved badly she would whisk me off to boarding school. And I suddenly and most violently did not want to do either.

I saw Richard's letters in quite a new light. Obviously he had been wretched because Aunt Laura was a narrow-minded stupid woman. He had just tried to be cheerful for my sake. And now she was coming to rescue me and I didn't want to be rescued.

It might have been different if Aunt Patsy had really wanted me to stay but why should she? I was an awful expense, I knew, and a nuisance, always being hungry and needing white shirts ironed for school and even help with my homework. And if she married Stephen I would be even more of a nuisance.

'Well, what do you think?' asked Aunt Patsy.

I took a gulp of my nearly cold coffee.

'I don't know,' I said limply.

We stared at each other across the kitchen table, with Aunty Patsy trying to discover my thoughts on the matter and I trying to find out what she really thought; but we didn't know each other well enough.

'Aunt Laura on the warpath,' said Aunt Patsy, 'coming to inspect me and see whether you keep regular hours, eat suitable food at stated intervals and meet my unsuitable friends! Grrr.'

At the remembrance of yesterday I couldn't help giggling, and Aunt Patsy giggled too. In fact we became quite uproarious and I spilt my coffee.

'Darling Emma,' said Aunt Patsy. 'I can't decide your future. You will have to decide yourself, though I think it's unfair when you're so young. But it would be even more unfair if I tried to decide for you. Do you understand?'

I nodded. I did, in a way. But I wished, all the same, that she would simply take charge and tell me what to do. Aunt Laura undoubtedly would and that was why I still had a sneaking feeling that life with her would be much simpler and more peaceful (if not quite so interesting) than life with Aunt Patsy.

Chapter Nine

I HAD quite a struggle before Aunt Patsy would let me go back to school on Monday.

'Are you sure you want to go?' she kept asking.

'Of course. I don't want to get behind.'

'Why you have this absurd addiction for exam-passing I'll never understand.'

'It's not just exams. I like school.'

'You're an unnatural child!'

'I think it would be much more unnatural not to like it,' I retorted.

'OK,' said Aunt Patsy smiling. 'You win. But if you have any trouble with that moronic charac-ter, let me know.'

'I won't,' I said confidently.

While I was waiting in the playground for the bell to ring some of the girls pounced on me.

'Where did you go?'

'I just went home,' I said loftily.

'Fancy making all that fuss about getting the belt.'

'I wasn't making a fuss. I just don't choose to have a horrible beefy old man like Mr Hamilton hitting me. Besides it was unfair. He has no business to terrorize us.'

'Of course it was,' said Elizabeth, linking her arm through mine. 'I think Emma was dead right. I wish I'd had the nerve.'

'Oscar would like a few words with you,' said one of the girls, mimicking Mr Hamilton. 'He's a real nit!'

'Can't teach for toffee.'

'I hate Maths anyway.'

'I wonder what he'll be like today.'

I was just going to boast about the awful things Aunt Patsy had told the headmaster and then I thought better of it.

Maths was third period but instead of Mr Hamilton our class teacher came in and introduced a student. She said Mr Hamilton was ill (I wonder if he really did have flu?) and that we were to be specially helpful and well-behaved to the student whose name was Miss Ogilvie.

She was young and thin and earnest and though we teased her a little – you can't somehow help it with students – we were pretty nice to her on the whole.

Nothing much else happened except that the Lady Adviser gave us one of her stupid lectures. She is a sort of matron who sees that everyone is clean and tidy; if someone has a headache she gives them an aspirin and lets them lie down for half an hour. She was always urging us to bring our little problems to her but of course we never did. Every few weeks she would give us a talk: about why we should wear school uniform, and be a credit to the school, and behave quietly on buses, and would warn us that girls wearing jazzy stockings would be sent home, and that if we modulated our voices and learnt to speak like ladies we'd all get much better jobs, and a lot of nonsense no one ever listened to.

This morning she found fault with Elizabeth's hair and stuck in two horrible kirby grips to keep it behind her ears. The moment she bustled through the door to lecture some other class Elizabeth promptly took them out again.

I went in to dinner with Elizabeth. I usually found it a bit difficult to talk to her because I didn't watch the telly and she was always describing to me the programme she'd seen the night before. But today we had Mr Hamilton to talk about and I told her, in confidence, how Aunt Patsy had torn into the headmaster. She was terribly impressed and kept saying, 'Jings, your aunt's got a nerve.'

'I wonder if he really has got flu,' I said.

'I think he's got the boot,' said Elizabeth.

Then when we were coming out of the dining-hall we ran into the History teacher. He stopped us and said: 'Emma and Elizabeth, just the girls I wanted to see. Can you spare me a moment?'

Of course we could, and he explained that there was going to be an exhibition of students' work at the end of the term and he wanted a pictorial chart made of medieval Scotland, with a plan of a village and a town and photographs of people and buildings and little pictures of this and that and an example of what an illuminated manuscript looked like.

'If you two could get together sometimes after school you might have a stab at it,' he said. 'Elizabeth is good at drawing and Emma's handwriting is a thing of beauty and a joy for ever. What do you say?'

'It might be fun,' I said cautiously, looking sideways at Elizabeth to see if she looked enthusiastic under her fringe.

'Now the thing is, do you live reasonably near each other and would your mothers let you gad round in the evening?'

'My mother wouldn't mind,' said Elizabeth quickly, 'as long as I'm home by ten.'

'Well, see if you can fix something up and then I'll give you the materials.'

He beamed at us both and strode off down the passage.

'Would your aunt mind?' Elizabeth asked me.

'No, of course not. She never minds!' I said proudly.

'Well, I'd ask you round to my place but there are kids all over and we wouldn't have peace to work. Could I come round to you?'

For a moment I felt a twinge; after all I had described Aunt Patsy's flat as an 'historic' house; and then I thought, well, after all, it *is* an historic house. As far as I could make out all the houses round there were historic.

'Come round after school and we'll ask my aunt if she'll lend us pens and paints and things.'

So Elizabeth came back with me. I wondered

what she'd say to the stairs but she didn't say anything. I hoped that it would be one of Aunt Patsy's good days and that she'd have tea ready, but she was working in her studio, wearing very grubby slacks and a huge black sweater, with an old shirt which she used instead of a proper painter's smock flapping round her shoulders. Her hair was on end and she had some paint on her cheek.

'This is Elizabeth,' I said and then I told her about the history project.

She was most helpful, promised a pen with a thick italic nib and some indian ink for the lettering but we'd jolly well have to find our own paints as she wasn't having hers mucked up. 'You'd better go and buy some,' she said, rootling in her bag and produced a scrumpled ten-shilling note.

'I have enough pocket money saved,' I said with dignity.

'Don't bite the hand that feeds you or look a gift horse in the mouth,' said Aunty Patsy.

'Can I give Elizabeth some tea?'

'Of course. Eat anything you like as long as you don't disturb me. I'm working at high pressure.'

She disappeared into her studio again and Elizabeth and I went into the kitchen.

'Gosh, your aunt's rather weird,' whispered Elizabeth – she had been staring at Aunt Patsy as if she had never seen anyone like her before.

'That's because she's an artist,' I said haughtily.

'Oh, I know. I didn't mean she wasn't nice.'

'What would you like for tea? Shall we have toasted cheese? And there may be some chocolate biscuits left.'

After tea I showed Elizabeth my room: she was very envious as she had to share with her little sister, but she couldn't get over us not having the telly.

'You can come round and watch ours if you like,' she offered.

After tea we went out and bought a paintbox and some brushes and some pencils and a big soft rubber and then I chummed her to the bus stop.

'Is your Mum getting better?' she asked while we waited for the bus.

'She's gone abroad,' I said quickly. 'She has to live in a warm climate.'

Then the bus came.

When I got home again I arranged my drawing materials on my desk but I felt lonely and wanted someone to talk to. I went up to the studio, knocked at the door and opened it.

'What is it now?' Aunt Patsy barked, looking up crossly from her drawing-board.

'I got the paintbox and things.'

'Good.'

'What are we going to have for supper?'

'You're not hungry again, are you?'

'Well, I soon will be.'

'Then for goodness sake, Emma, go and stuff yourself, but please, please, please leave me alone until I've finished this.'

I hesitated and then to my disgust found myself saying in a whiney voice.

'I wish we had the telly.'

'Well, we haven't and we're not going to. I loathe and abominate it.'

'All the girls at school have sets.'

'Emma! Scram!'

I scrammed. I shut the door with a bang, and stamped down the stairs and went into the kitchen. Of course I wasn't hungry. I just wanted to talk. How beastly Aunt Patsy was. I sat and glowered out of the window at the roofs and chimney-pots and hated everyone. I wished, oh how I wished that everything was different. It was difficult not to cry and I was just getting that chokey feeling in my throat and hot feeling behind my eyes when the doorbell rang. It was Stephen.

He just said, 'Hullo chick,' and bounded up the stairs into the studio, and I hated him too. 'She'll have time to talk to him,' I thought and felt even more aggrieved.

But within two minutes he had bounded down again.

'Why didn't you tell me Patsy was working?' he asked me ruefully.

'You didn't give me time.'

'Grrr,' he said. 'Patsy's a menace when she's trying to meet a deadline. She flew at me like a wild cat.'

'She flew at me too,' I admitted. We grinned at each other.

'She promised I could come to supper and she's completely forgotten,' Stephen grumbled.

'I could make you some supper,' I said, cheering up.

'Could you really?'

'If eggs and bacon would do? I can't find anything else.'

'Eggs and bacon would suit me admirably. Now, tell me, what happened at school today? Is the monster still in evidence?'

I told him about the student, what the girls had said, and about the pictorial history, and he said he had some material that might be useful. So we ate our bacon and eggs and chatted like mad.

At about nine o'clock Aunt Patsy appeared, kissed Stephen as if nothing had happened, and said: 'Emma, I'm starving to death. What have you two been guzzling? Can I have some too?'

I thought Aunt Patsy might have apologized, and that Stephen might have pointed out that it was very rude to invite someone for supper and then forget, but neither of them mentioned it.

So I found some more bacon and eggs and

cooked her a big plateful. Then I decided I would have a bath and go to bed.

'Don't forget the washing-up,' I said as I left them, getting my own back at last.

Chapter Ten

THE next couple of weeks passed pleasantly although Mr Hamilton did come back. He was much the same, except that he ignored me completely. But when he found one of the boys, Thomas Macintyre, reading a comic under his desk, instead of belting him there and then he said:

'I understand that some of our more sensitive scholars do not care for encounters with Oscar. How do you feel about it, Thomas?'

Thomas wriggled and muttered:

'I don't know, sir.'

'You don't know, Thomas? You don't know if you would prefer six words with Oscar to, let us say, an hour's extra homework?'

'Gie's the belt, sir,' Thomas said, going scarlet with embarrassment.

'No, Thomas. Curiously enough my intention is not to consider your wishes. If you study comics when you ought to be studying algebra it seems only right that you should study algebra when you might be titillating your imagination with stories of spacemen and private eyes. Take problems 7 to 13, inclusive, please Thomas, to redress the balance.'

Of course Thomas was furious, and he and several other boys made rude remarks to me during break but the girls were on my side, especially Elizabeth.

We had become friends. We had been working on our history project off and on. Stephen found us a nice bit of illuminated manuscript to copy, with a capital letter entwined with birds and flowers and a strip at the bottom of funny little men shooting a deer with bows and arrows. I copied the lettering and Elizabeth did the pictures and it looked splendid.

I also went down the hill to Stockbridge to her house to watch the telly. So I was able to discuss with the girls who was fabulous in the Top Twenty and what we thought was going to happen in the serial.

Elizabeth was a peculiar girl. Her mother liked her to wear nice clothes, frocks or frilly blouses and skirts but she liked to wear scruffy jeans and big jerseys. So she used to put her old clothes in a duffel bag and dive into the nearest public lavatory to change whenever she went out. I thought she was bonkers!

She lived in a super new block of flats, and she and her family – three younger sisters and a jolly fat baby – were always sitting together cosily in the kitchen watching telly and drinking cups of tea.

Her mother was quite nice except she would keep asking Elizabeth why she didn't wear her hair short like mine.

'But it's the fashion, Mum,' Elizabeth would explain hopelessly, and I would chip in: 'You can't wear curly hair long – it would make me look like a spaniel. But long straight hair is super.'

'I think it looks a proper mess,' her mother would snort.

Elizabeth had a thing on one of the boy prefects. She was always hanging about the corridors hoping to catch sight of him or planning to sit next to him in the bus. Once at the bus stop a pencil fell out of her school bag and he actually picked it up. She talked about it for weeks. I couldn't understand what she saw in him: he had awful sticky-out ears and his name was Gilbert.

One evening when she'd been at my house she said: 'Let's knock off early, Emma. There's a smashing coffee bar I'm dying to go to. But I can't go alone.'

'I'll make you some coffee,' I suggested.

'No, I want to go out. But you must chum me.'

'Oh all right.'

Aunt Patsy was out and I thought maybe I ought to leave her a note but then I thought, why bother? She probably wouldn't even notice.

So we went to this coffee bar. It was all furnished in wood, and there was a juke-box, and the air was full of steam and cigarette smoke. The people were mostly teenagers: boys with floppy hair that they were always combing; and now I understood about Elizabeth because all the girls there looked the same. I felt a bit odd myself wearing a skirt and having short hair.

We stood in a queue to get our coffee, and Elizabeth led the way to a table. I realized then why she had wanted to come. Gilbert was sitting at the next table.

Of course she was dying to talk to him but she was far too shy so she just sat, with her hair hiding her face, sipping her coffee and making the odd remark.

'Lend us a threepenny bit,' she said at last. 'I want to play *You're the only girl.*'

'OK.'

She got up very slowly and walked over to the juke-box, waited until the record dropped into place, and walked slowly back again, all the time stealing glances at Gilbert from under her fringe. I suffered for her because Gilbert was talking to a couple of other boys and took no notice at all.

'If you're lonely, girl, remember that you're the only girl for me,' sang the juke-box.

Then just as Elizabeth was level with his table Gilbert looked up, smiled at her and said, 'Hi.'

That was the only thing he said to her until we left, and then he said, 'Chow' (which is what a lot of people were saying at that time), but I could tell Elizabeth was as pleased as punch.

'Fancy him being there,' she kept saying as we waited at the bus stop. 'Fancy him noticing me. Fancy him speaking to me.'

'You're a nut case,' I told her. 'An absolute out and out nut case.'

'I know Emma, but he's so gorgeous.'

'Here's your bus, goodnight.'

'Goodnight, and thanks for coming.'

The lighted bus swung down the street with

Elizabeth waving frantically and I walked back up the hill home, chuckling to myself. I hoped I'd never get that way about a boy, especially one with sticky-out ears called Gilbert.

When I opened the front door Aunt Patsy literally pounced on me.

'Emma, where have you been? It's terribly late.'

'I've just been with Elizabeth to a coffee bar,' I explained. 'I didn't realize it was so late.'

'It's half past ten,' Aunt Patsy exploded. 'I came back an hour ago and there wasn't a sign of you. I've been worried stiff.'

I stared at her in absolute amazement. Aunt Patsy worried stiff! I could hardly believe my ears. I didn't realize she even knew the meaning of the word 'late'.

Recently we had been getting on rather well together. Of course, she still forgot my pocket-money and snapped my head off if I interrupted her when she was working; and I still grumbled about not having a telly and she would complain about my always being hungry; but this was somehow more natural and friendly than our polite stage. Still she had never fussed or made me feel I had to ask her permission to do anything – I just told her. I think she must have noticed my surprise because she calmed down and murmured sheepishly: 'You might have left a note.'

'I'm terribly sorry.'

'Well, don't do it again.'

'I promise. I just never thought.'

'I never thought either,' began Aunt Patsy and then changed what she was going to say. 'Was it fun in the coffee bar?'

So I told her about Elizabeth and she laughed like anything.

Although it was so late I lay thinking for a long time before I went to sleep. The wind was whooshing round the gable end so that I felt as if I were living in a lighthouse with the sea surging all round. I liked lying there with the eiderdown pulled under my chin, listening to the wind, and I listed all the reasons why I was happy.

I had got used to Aunt Patsy's way of life and now even liked it: the way she didn't try to 'bring me up' but treated me as an equal, and how, if I was working on my history chart, she never interrupted to ask me to go out and buy some eggs or make coffee. I could stay up if I felt sociable or go to bed if I felt sleepy; I could bring Elizabeth home when I wanted and go out when I wanted. (Leaving a note to say where I'd gone was completely different from having to ask permission.) I liked our movable meal-times, so that sometimes we had breakfast at lunch-time and supper any time from six o'clock to midnight. I had even got used to living up the terrible stairs in Castlehill, and I actually liked the crumbly old Royal Mile (though I still thought it ought to be tidied up as soon as possible). In a way, it was rather marvellous to be in the middle of so much history. I used to wander into the wynds and closes and wonder what James Boswell and David Hume and Robert Burns had been like, what clothes they had worn and what they had talked about. No wonder Mary, Queen of Scots had been depressed, I thought, living in gloomy old Holyrood Palace with the mist sliding over Arthur's Seat wishing she could go home to France. And I definitely liked school. It was fun being near the top of the class, and trying to outwit Mr Hamilton, and finding new things for the history chart, and being friends with Elizabeth.

Of course I still missed Mother and Father but it didn't hurt so much. It was rather as if they had gone away, and I could think my thoughts as if I were writing them a letter, and they would understand and be pleased with me.

Just as I was dropping off to sleep I remembered Aunt Laura's visit. But I said firmly to myself, 'I'll think about that tomorrow.'

Chapter Eleven

WHEN I did come to think about Aunt Laura I decided the only person who would understand my feelings was Richard. So the next evening, after I'd finished my homework, I wrote him a long letter.

Dear Richard,

I've changed my mind and don't say, Ha ha, girls always do. I really want to stay with Aunt Patsy. I've got used to everything now and even like it. But the awful thing is I don't know if Aunt Patsy wants me to stay. She and Stephen are going to get married at Christmas but she never says things like 'when we're married we'll all do such and such,' or tells me if we're going to go on living in Castlehill, or what will happen to me if they go away on a honeymoon. If only Aunt Laura's letter hadn't arrived at the exact moment it did I would have been able to ask all these questions, but now I simply can't. Aunt Patsy does appear to like me but that is different from her wanting me to go on staying after she is married. Perhaps she is just waiting for Aunt Laura to carry me off so that she and Stephen can be left in peace.

The other evening something most peculiar happened. I went out with a friend to a coffee bar and when I got home Aunt Patsy, who usually doesn't care a hoot where I am or what I'm doing, was furious. She said she was worried about me! I still can't make up my mind if it was because she is fond of me or because I'm a nuisance.

I don't think I could bear to be uprooted again and have to start getting used to someone else's ways. And I don't think I like the sound of Aunt Laura.

Richard wrote back that I wasn't to worry, and he was sure that if I was happy, Aunt Patsy must be happy too because, living so closely together as we did, I couldn't have been happy if Aunt Patsy hadn't felt the same.

It wasn't a very satisfactory letter!

So I started worrying all over again. How ought I to behave during Aunt Laura's visit so that she would let me stay in Edinburgh? If I behaved too nicely, and was tidy and polite, and went to bed early she might think I would 'fit in' with her family. And if I was very noisy and teen-age-ish, and played pop records very loudly, and left all the towels on the bathroom floor, she might insist that I was immediately packed away to a good boarding school.

Suppose, too, that Aunt Patsy was in one of her working moods, wearing her old slacks with her hair on end, and forgot about meals, and invited Stephen's friends to a noisy party. And suppose Stephen used bad language or forgot to shave, and he and Aunt Patsy had one of their conversations about the stupidity of the educational system.

It was all terribly worrying: I almost stopped feeling hungry and, when I went to bed, I tossed and turned as I imagined all the things that could go wrong with the visit.

Aunt Laura wrote that she was coming for the weekend and would get in touch after her arrival on the Friday. When Aunt Patsy read the letter aloud to me I felt a horrible thud at the bottom of my stomach.

All that day at school I couldn't concentrate and the teachers accused me of wool-gathering and told me that if I didn't pay more attention, I'd fail my exams.

When school finished I didn't know whether to hurry home to see if Aunt Laura had arrived or to hang around and put off knowing the worst for a little longer. However, there was a nice prefect at the bus stop who actually kept the queue in order, and stopped the boys from pushing the girls out of their way; so I got on an early bus, and the church clock at the corner was just striking four as I began very slowly to climb the stairs.

I remembered that first morning I had climbed them: how disgusted I'd been at the way the stairs sagged in the middle, at the paint flaking off the walls, and at the peculiar musty smell. And now I didn't mind at all. I hardly noticed.

When I reached the last flight I heard the sound of a piano being played. Now sometimes Aunt Patsy did play the piano but she wasn't very good, and this was fast ripply sort of playing, quite different from hers. I thought it must be the radio but while I was taking off my coat I saw the transistor on the kitchen table: so it couldn't be the radio.

I rushed upstairs and burst into the studio, hardly daring to hope; but I was quite right! There, sitting at the piano with his copper head bent over the keys, looking perfectly at home, was Richard.

'Richard!' I squeaked, rushing at him, and completely forgetting that boys don't like being hugged. But he didn't seem to mind and hugged me back, and then we both looked at Aunt Patsy who was curled up on the sofa, smiling at us.

'Richard just got here about an hour ago,' she said. 'I must say, you play the piano remarkably well, Richard.'

'It's a nice piano,' said Richard, 'but it needs tuning.' He did a quick little arpeggio and shuddered.

I looked at Aunt Patsy to see if she thought he was being rude but she seemed to think he was quite right to tell her, and promised to get it seen to directly.

I thought how like both of them it was to be talking about pianos and music instead of any of the questions that people usually ask: where he should sleep, if he had eaten lately, and why he hadn't rung up. I suspected she hadn't even asked whether he had had permission from Aunt Laura to come or had merely walked out of the house. Aunt Patsy seemed to take it for granted that it was all the most natural thing in the world.

But I didn't.

'How did you get here? Why have you come? Does Aunt Laura know? When did you get here? Oh Richard!' I was quite breathless and silly with excitement.

'I hitch-hiked,' said Richard calmly, 'on an overnight lorry. I'm not having family conferences taking place behind my back.'

'But does Aunt Laura know?'

'I don't think she does because I left after she did. Oh, it's all right. The police won't be scouring the countryside for me. I left a note in the approved fashion.'

'On a pincushion?' giggled Aunt Patsy.

'No, on the hall table.'

'That was sensible.'

'I must say I hope I never have to be a long-distance lorry driver,' said Richard. 'You have to sit all bent up like a hairpin and the engine makes so much noise it practically deafens you. And the food at transport cafés is absolutely vile.'

'Talking about food,' said Aunt Patsy, 'shall we have some?'

'Gorgeous idea,' said Richard. 'I don't suppose you have a horse, but I could certainly eat one.'

So we all went down to the kichen. Fortunately it was one of Aunt Patsy's good days and there were plenty of things in the fridge and the cupboard.

Aunt Patsy cooked onion soup which made us all cry, and while the onions were sizzling in butter Richard grated cheese to put in it. I opened a tin of ham and made a huge salad with curly lettuce and watercress and thin slivers of cucumber. To make quite sure it would be enough I opened a tin of pineapple and added chunks of that.

Soon we were all sitting round the kitchen table, eating and talking like mad, about Edinburgh, and my school and Mr Hamilton, and whether the Scottish National Orchestra was any good, and Richard's school, and his chances of a scholarship, and Aunt Patsy's tiles, and my history project.

The only thing we didn't talk about was Aunt Laura.

After we had finished, Richard was still hungry so he topped up with brown bread and cheese.

'I see big appetites run in the family!' said Aunt Patsy. 'Can I press you to a chocolate biscuit, Richard?'

'I wouldn't say no,' Richard said, wiping the crumbs off his mouth.

'Then we'll take some upstairs with our coffee,' Aunt Patsy suggested. 'And perhaps – if you're quite sure you've eaten enough, Richard – you might play us some more music. That is, unless the piano's really too awful.'

'It isn't that bad,' admitted Richard. 'Compared with Aunt Laura's it's a marvel.'

When he had finished playing he sat down on the sofa, and began yawning and yawning and yawning. Then quite suddenly he was asleep.

'How stupid of me!' exclaimed Aunt Patsy. 'I'd forgotten he'd been up all night.'

So we arranged him on the sofa with a pillow under his head. We couldn't help giggling while Aunt Patsy loosened his tie and edged his shoes off: he felt so limp and funny, but he was so fast asleep he didn't wake up. Then Aunt Patsy fetched a couple of rugs to keep him warm when we turned off the fire.

'What a nice brother you have,' she whispered as we tiptoed downstairs. 'How dreadfully you must have missed him!'

I nodded. I didn't feel I needed to speak.

Chapter Twelve

WHEN I woke up next morning I heard Richard playing the piano again and I hoped Aunt Patsy wouldn't be cross at being disturbed. It was lovely to lie in bed and to know that we would have a whole day together. The sun had just arrived round the corner of Arthur's Seat, and I could see the golden glow in the sky from my bed. It was actually going to be a fine day.

But I couldn't lie still for long. I jumped out of bed, dressed and washed, and started frying large quantities of bacon for breakfast. Richard came in looking sleek and well-brushed.

'Do I smell bacon?' he asked. 'I thought so. It's my favourite smell first thing in the morning. How efficient you are!'

'Somebody has to be,' I retorted smartly.

Then Aunt Patsy came in yawning in her dressing gown.

'Do you have to play the piano so early in the morning, Richard?' she asked.

'Well I do rather,' said Richard smiling.

'I suppose I should be grateful it wasn't boogie-woogie.'

'Honestly, Aunt Patsy!' I said. 'No one plays boogie-woogie nowadays. It's terribly old-fashioned.'

After breakfast we sat around talking and Richard examined some of Aunt Patsy's designs and my history chart until Aunt Patsy broke it up.

'Delightful though all this social life is, I must get down to work, and you two are a distracting influence. Why don't you go out and see the town? And if I provide the wherewithal you can eat lunch out and leave me in peace till tea-time.'

'Good-oh!' said Richard.

So we spent the day exploring Edinburgh. We climbed the stairs to the Outlook Tower where a camera throws an enlarged picture of the city on to a circular white screen; we poked our noses into all the courts and wynds, and visited all the museums in the Royal Mile

We didn't go into Holyrood Palace because you have to go on a conducted tour and the guide tells you hundreds and hundreds of names and dates. Instead we climbed Salisbury Crags. I stuck to the path but Richard couldn't resist showing off his rock climbing which made me nervous though I didn't dare say so.

From the top you can see for miles: fields, woods, hills, blue sea, and the whole city spread out below like the view from an aeroplane.

Richard is usually rather solemn and grown-up but sometimes he goes mad and behaves as if he were a ten-year-old. Suddenly he whooped like an Indian and began racing down the hill. 'Come on, Emma,' he shouted. 'Let's run all the way down.'

'You're crazy,' I shouted after him. There were a lot of loose stones which you could easily trip over and I had no intention of falling on my nose.

He was sitting on a rock when I panted up to him.

'I think Edinburgh's fabulous,' he said.

'It is rather.'

'I wonder if I should go to the University here, that is, if there's a good music department.'

'Oh do!' – and then I remembered – 'What about Aunt Laura?'

'I refuse to think about Aunt Laura on a lovely day like this. She's not going to run my life whatever she thinks.'

'I'm afraid she's going to run mine,' I muttered miserably.

'Nonsense!'

'Well, she is our guardian.'

'She needs,' said Richard grandly, 'a little handling, that's all.'

I told him my idea of acting the 'Terrible Teenager' but he shut me up.

'Don't be such a nit, Emma. Be yourself. It's the only way. Besides, you're a lousy actress. You couldn't keep it up for ten minutes.'

'But—' I began.

'But me no buts. Aunt Laura is Forbidden Topic number one. Besides I'm hungry. Let's go and find some grub.'

We found a rather nasty café and ate fish and chips, and ice cream. Then we went for a walk in Princes Street Gardens. The gardeners were brushing up the fallen leaves, and there was the bitter-sweet autumnal smell of a bonfire. The north slope of the gardens was in shadow but there was still enough sun to catch the castle rock and turn it pink. Although we could hear the roar of the traffic at the West End and a diesel train hooting Whoo-hoo as it went into the tunnel, the gardens seemed very peaceful.

I should have liked to stay but it was too cold and I shivered.

'Shall we plod homewards now?' asked Richard. 'It'll be tea-time by the time we get back.'

So we crossed the little humped railway bridge and after we had puffed up the long hill home I was quite warm again.

When we got back there was the sound of voices coming from the studio, and when we opened the door there were Aunt Laura and Aunt Patsy having tea together.

Richard was as calm as a cucumber, shook hands politely, and then sat down and poured himself some tea. I, however, stopped short, blushing furiously and wishing I could fall through a hole in the floor.

Aunt Laura rose to her feet and made a swoop at me. She pressed me to her bosom, and actually

began sniffling down my neck and saying, 'You poor child!' I was absolutely furious and extricated myself as soon as I could, mumbled that I was fine, thank you, and stood there feeling an utter fool.

'Come and have some tea, Emma,' said Aunt Patsy, and I saw by the glint in her eye and the curl of her lip that she was as disgusted with Aunt Laura's behaviour as I was. So I sat down and accepted a cup of tea, but my hand shook so much that I nearly spilt it.

'I didn't expect to find you here, Richard,' said Aunt Laura, sitting down too.

'I acted on impulse,' said Richard in a lordly way.

'It's not usually considered good manners to descend on people without warning,' Aunt Laura said severely.

I thought Richard was going to snap back but Aunt Patsy smoothly intervened.

'Oh, Richard has always had a standing invitation,' she said. 'I'm only sorry he didn't come before. Do have a piece of cake, Laura.'

By this time I had calmed down, and I noticed several surprising things. The room was beautifully tidy. The tea was served in the best tea service (instead of mugs), and there was actually a clean cloth on the table. There was cake and little sandwiches, a knife for the butter and jam in a little dish instead of the jam pot. And Aunt Patsy herself was dressed in a dark wool frock, her face was nicely made-up, and her hair like a smooth dark helmet. She looked absolutely respectable.

And then I realized why. She wanted me to stay with her! She wanted to impress Aunt Laura that she was a fit and proper person to look after me.

I wanted to shout Hooray, and jump up and hug her but, of course, I couldn't. I just looked across at her and gave her an enormous grin.

Meanwhile Aunt Laura asked me questions.

'And how do you like Edinburgh, Emma?'

'I love it,' I said happily.

'And how are you doing at school?'

'Quite well, I think. It was a bit queer at first but I like it now.'

'There's a very good girls' school in Exeter,' said Aunt Laura.

'Edinburgh schools are famous,' said Aunt Patsy hypocritically. 'And I've had very good reports of Emma's work from the headmaster.'

'I'm glad you have made such a good adjustment,' said Aunt Laura. 'And I'm sure you, Patsy, have had to make an adjustment too. Girls of Emma's age are not always easy to handle.'

'Emma doesn't need handling,' said Aunt Patsy.

'Still I think we should speak frankly,' said Aunt Laura. 'Young girls do need a stable family life as a background.'

'There's nothing particularly unstable about my life,' said Aunt Patsy, with a trace of acid in her voice. 'In actual fact I'm getting married at Christmas.'

'My dear Patsy, congratulations!' exclaimed

Aunt Laura. 'I'm so happy for you. And who is the lucky man?'

'His name is Stephen McTaggart. He lectures at the Art College, and is Art Editor for a magazine called *Scottish Homes*.'

'Then that clarifies everything,' said Aunt Laura. 'Obviously a newly-married couple don't want—' she paused delicately.

'On the contrary,' retorted Aunt Patsy. 'This newly-married couple does want. We want very much. I've talked about it to Stephen and he thinks it's a marvellous idea to start off with a bit of ready-made family.'

'Still, I do feel,' said Aunt Laura, 'that in my position as guardian I should accept the responsibility of Emma's upbringing. I'm sure she will be very happy with us in Exeter.'

Here Richard interrupted. 'I think, if you don't mind my butting in, that you should ask Emma what she wants.'

'A child may know what she wants but does she know what is best for her?' demanded Aunt Laura.

'Just what objection exactly do you have to her staying with me?' demanded Aunt Patsy with an edge to her voice.

'My dear Patsy, there's no need to be offended. I only referred to your lack of experience. After all, you've never been married and had children of your own. And I don't feel that all these artistic people you mix with—' again she paused.

I was almost in despair. How could anyone prove they were right in such an argument. I could see the glitter in Aunt Patsy's eyes which meant she was really angry and even Richard looked pink. At any moment now someone was going to be rude. But when Aunt Patsy spoke again her voice was as smooth as silk.

'Don't let's argue, Laura,' she said. 'I know we're very different people—'

'That's why Emma should decide,' broke in Richard. 'After all, what you both want is for her to be happy and even if she is only thirteen she's a jolly sensible thirteen. It's horrible to be argued over.'

'Of course it's up to Emma,' agreed Aunt Patsy quickly, giving me a smile.

Aunt Laura sighed and tightened her lips. 'Well, Emma?' she said pompously.

What I wanted to do was to burst into tears and scream that I wanted to stay with Aunt Patsy and that no one, no one, no one would ever take me away and that I loathed Aunt Laura and the thought of going to Exeter. But now I saw that this was childish and stupid. Richard had said I was old enough to make up my own mind but I had to do it politely and tactfully. I took a deep breath.

'It's terribly kind of you, Aunt Laura, to offer to have me in Exeter,' I said, 'and I'd love to come and visit you some time. But, honestly, I do feel I've settled down now, and I love living here with Aunt Patsy, and if she and Stephen won't find me a nuisance, then please let me stay.'

I smiled at Aunt Laura as I spoke. I suppose I had been turning her into a monster in my imagination but now I saw she was quite an ordinary well-meaning woman who probably did want me to be happy. Anyhow, she smiled back and said:

'If that's the way you feel, dear, then of course there's no more to say. But I must say it's rather surprising. I never thought of you having maternal feelings, Patsy.'

'They're not maternal feelings, just auntly feelings!' said Aunty Patsy.

Just then the doorbell rang.

'That will be Stephen,' said Aunt Patsy, and I ran down to let him in.

'Has she arrived?' he whispered.

'Yes, and everything's all right. I'm going to stay with you.'

'Goodie, goodie,' whispered Stephen, squeezing my arm. 'Now I must go and be polite. How do you think I look?'

He was actually wearing a dark suit and a clean white shirt; he was beautifully shaved, and had had his hair cut. He, too, looked absolutely respectable.

'Smashing,' I said. 'For once.'

He gave me a quick cuff. 'Don't be cheeky.'

He came upstairs and was introduced. We had some sherry and everyone made polite conversation but I didn't bother to listen. I was too busy making plans. At last Aunt Laura said she must go back to her hotel. She kissed me again and said she did hope that everything would work out for the best, and that I must write often and tell her how I was getting on.

The moment the front door had clicked shut Richard sat down at the piano and played a wild polka, while Aunt Patsy, Stephen and I danced round the room singing all sorts of words to the music.

'That's the way to treat Aunt Laura – that's the way to treat them all – Aunt Laura's through the door-O – and we can have a ball.'

'Thank goodness, now I can relax,' said Aunt Patsy, taking off her shoes and falling back on the sofa laughing.

'I told you so,' said Richard to me.

'I hardly recognized you,' said Stephen to Aunt Patsy.

'I hardly recognized you!'

'Let's have a picnic supper,' said Aunt Patsy. 'I'm so exhausted at being a stable family background I couldn't lift a finger. Richard and Emma, do you think you could bring up everything edible you can find in the fridge, and we'll be messy and—' she looked at me doubtfully. 'Or do you want to go on being respectable?'

I hesitated for a moment. After all it would be rather nice to have an elegant supper. Then I thought, 'What did it matter? What matters is that we're all together, and we'll laugh and talk and enjoy ourselves, and make plans. There'll be lots of other opportunities for elegant suppers.'

'I don't mind a picnic,' I said, 'but I insist on the tea things being washed up first.'

Richard groaned. 'As far as I'm concerned your

appeal falls on deaf ears,' he said. 'Don't be such a fanatic.'

But I didn't reply. I just carried the tea things downstairs to the kitchen.